DATE DUE

AUG 3 0 2018			
			PRINTED IN U.S.A.

THE BLANK CANVAS

THE BLANK CANVAS

GLEN EBISCH

FIVE STAR
A part of Gale, Cengage Learning

GALE
CENGAGE Learning·

Farmington Hills, Mich • San Francisco • New York • Waterville, Maine
Meriden, Conn • Mason, Ohio • Chicago

IBRARY OF CONGRESS CATALOGING-IN-PUBLICATION DATA

Ebisch, Glen Albert, 1946–
    The blank canvas / Glen Ebisch.
      pages cm.
    ISBN-13: 978-1-4328-2818-9 (hardcover)
    ISBN-10: 1-4328-2818-5 (hardcover)
    1. Art museums—New Jersey—Fiction. 2. Artists—Crimes against—Fiction. 3. Murder—Investigation—Fiction. I. Title.
    PS3605.B57B53 2014
    813'.6—dc23   2013041353

First Edition. First Printing: April 2014
Find us on Facebook– https://www.facebook.com/FiveStarCengage
Visit our website– http://www.gale.cengage.com/fivestar/
Contact Five Star™ Publishing at FiveStar@cengage.com

Printed in the United States of America
1 2 3 4 5 6 7 18 17 16 15 14

THE BLANK CANVAS

CHAPTER 1

I stood in the room surrounded by art, or at least some of it was art. There are people who would have stood frozen with indecision trying to decide which was which. Not me. My motto, a reversal of the old saying, is "I may not know what I like, but I know what's art." The paintings to my right of precarious sand dunes, flying loons, perky sandpipers, romantic sunsets and crashing waves were my idea of non-art. The works to my left consisting of abstract forms, blobs of color, and streaks of light were art.

You say you disagree with me. Well, Miranda Gould, my supervisor, certainly did. In fact, she was looking with undisguised disdain on our newest acquisition, which was an all-white canvas with a small rectangle in the middle painted in a slightly darker shade of white. The overall impression was one of . . . well . . . whiteness.

"How do you know which end is up?" Miranda asked.

I pointed to tiny arrows painted in two of the corners, one pointing up, the other down. "I think the artist has helped us there."

"That's really tacky."

I shook my head. "It shows he has a sense of humor. He's making an ironic postmodern comment on modern art by suggesting that it's wide open to a wealth of interpretations."

Miranda gave my reply some thought. "Phooey," she finally responded. "He just wanted to make sure it got hung the way he wanted."

I shrugged and looked at the signature in the lower right corner. It said "Rafferty."

"I've never heard of him," I remarked.

"We've sold a few of his over the past couple of years." Miranda propped the painting up on an easel and glared at it. "They all look pretty much the same to me."

I wasn't sure whether that was her own considered opinion of modern art, or whether it was at least partly influenced by her boyfriend, one of the more prolific producers of acrylic paintings of pipers and plovers.

"But don't get me wrong," Miranda continued, "I'm glad you can find something positive to say about this kind of stuff. I'd reached the point where I couldn't pretend to like it, even when a customer was interested. That's why I told Mr. Tompkins he had to hire an assistant for the summer who knew something about pictures that don't really look like anything."

"Nonrepresentational art," I added helpfully.

"Whatever. It was just luck you were available."

Luck it certainly was. When I got the call from a former coworker of mine asking me if I'd be interested in the job, I was thrilled. I had been feeling the need for some time away from my job as Auntie Mabel, an advice columnist for *The Ravensford Chronicle*, a local paper in western Massachusetts.

Roger St. Clair, the owner of the paper and my grandmother's boyfriend, agreed to give me the summer off, partly out of generosity and partly because he and my grandmother were planning to move into her house together. This was where I was currently staying, so now they would have the entire summer to get settled in before my return, assuming I ever did return. In fact, Roger was so happy to see me go, he was footing the bill for a very nice condo right across from the beach here in Safe Harbor, New Jersey, near the southern tip of the state. As for me, I was enjoying the opportunity to work at the Tompkins Gallery, and be back in the art world again, however peripherally.

The door opened and Harold Krass slipped inside. He had a way of insinuating himself into places. You'd look up and suddenly he'd be there, as though he had flowed through the walls by osmosis. He claimed it was a skill born of many years spent sneaking up on birds in order to photograph them for future painting.

Miranda ran across the room and stood up on her toes to kiss Harold, who happens to be her boyfriend. I wondered how she even found his lips amidst the efflorescence of beard that seemed to cover all but his forehead. He was quite tall and very thin, while Miranda was even shorter than my five-six and somewhat stocky. They made a visually interesting couple. I had thought he was close to sixty when we'd first met because his beard was liberally sprinkled with gray, but Miranda later assured me he was only three years older than her own age of forty. She thought the beard made him look mature. I thought it made him look like one of those crazed trappers common in old westerns with the slightly mad glint in his eyes, which he was currently casting across to the other side of the room where his pictures were on display.

"You haven't sold the painting of the flying gull yet?" he asked in an aggrieved tone.

"We've only had it for three days, darling," Miranda said.

Tough as nails with everyone else, she became all soft and gooey around Harold. Living proof of the extremes women will go to when it comes to keeping a man—any man.

"And we just sold your last picture of a gull seven days ago," I pointed out. "We may have saturated the gull market for a few weeks."

Harold gave me a hard look to see if I was being sarcastic. I kept my expression blank.

"That picture was nothing like this one." Harold went over and pointed to the bird's head. "See!"

I stared but had no clue what he was getting at. I glanced at Miranda, but she had the nervous smile on her face that she gets when Harold is making even less sense than usual.

"I'm sorry," I said, admitting defeat.

He sighed deeply to demonstrate his response to a world in which unobservant fools surrounded him.

"This gull is facing to the right. The one you sold two weeks ago was facing left."

"Now, I see," I said, resisting the impulse to roll my eyes.

Harold nodded solemnly. "That changes the entire perspective of the painting."

"Yes, this one has an entirely different perspective," Miranda echoed.

"Yeah, thanks for pointing that out," I said, just managing to keep the sarcasm out of my voice once again.

Miranda touched his arm. "Don't worry, honey, I'm sure we'll sell it over the weekend when there are more tourists around."

Harold nodded, as if he expected nothing less.

Miranda was probably right. Since it was still early June, the true shore season hadn't started up yet. Memorial Day was the symbolic start, but only with the closing of school toward the end of June would the tourists start to come in ever-greater waves until the end of August. They would soon fill the rows of Victorians that lined the streets around the pedestrian mall where our shop was located, eventually spreading to the hotels and condominium apartments that looked out onto the beach. Right now the weekend crowds of day-trippers were a small indication of what was soon to come. I hoped so because, although I received a small salary, my earnings needed to be supplemented by the commission I made on each artwork sold. So far I'd had to dig into my meager savings in order to live.

Harold made a coughing sound that I had eventually learned was his version of a laugh.

"At least I'm sure it will sell before that *thing*." He pointed smugly at the Rafferty.

I was tempted to tell him that the Rafferty was worth more than a whole flock of his bird paintings, but I knew I couldn't change his mind and there was no point in antagonizing my boss's boyfriend.

I glanced up, looking out through the store window that Miranda and I took turns keeping spotless; a man was standing there looking in at me. I felt a little shiver down my spine at being watched while unaware. The man walked up to the front door and came inside. Although it was a warm day, and most people sported shorts and t-shirts, he was wearing a three-piece suit made of wool. His head was covered with wispy gray hair. I guessed him to be in his seventies.

"That painting," he said, standing in front of me and pointing over my shoulder. "Is that a Rafferty?"

"Yes. And isn't it a fine example of formalism? Notice the—"

"I want to buy it," the man said softly but firmly.

I heard a sound behind me that might have been Harold's jaw hitting the floor.

CHAPTER 2

"You want to buy it," I repeated stupidly.

"Yes. It is for sale, isn't it?" He looked at me patiently with a gentle smile on his lips.

"Of course," I said. I glanced at Miranda to see if she wanted to take over. When we were both in the shop, we tried to take turns making sales, and I had made the last sale yesterday. She rolled her eyes wildly, which I interpreted to mean she wasn't about to sell a Rafferty with Harold standing there looking like he was in the process of having a stroke.

"How much is it?"

Since we hadn't completed displaying the painting, there was no price attached to the canvas. Mr. Tompkins, the owner of the studio, always set the prices. He would send a list to Miranda along with the paintings. I stared at Miranda, who eventually recovered enough to run over to her desk and find the latest price list.

"Twenty thousand," she announced.

Harold's expression became even more despondent, and I was sure that somewhere within that beard, his mouth was turned down in the opposite of a smiley face.

"That's fine," the man said, drawing a checkbook out of his inside jacket pocket.

The door opened and a couple came in. The woman was in her thirties and slender, wearing a pretty yellow sundress. The man, who might have been a few years older, had a sizeable belly confined by a tight polo shirt. His shorts were buckled below the expanse of his waist.

"Is that a Rafferty?" he asked in a harsh voice.

"Yes," I replied, wondering when Rafferty had become a household name on the level of Picasso.

"Well, my wife and I would like to buy it."

"I'm sorry, it's already been sold," the older man said.

The man in shorts paused for a moment, taking in the scene.

"I see you haven't written a check yet. That means the sale hasn't been finalized." He turned to me. "How much is he paying for it?"

"Twenty thousand," I said.

"I'll pay twenty-five."

"I'll pay thirty," the older man countered.

"I'll go up to thirty-five," the other man said.

I raised a hand in the air indicating that I wanted silence. "This isn't an auction house. This gentleman and I have already come to an agreement," I said, indicating the older man. "He gets the painting for the agreed twenty thousand."

The man in shorts turned to the older man. "I'll give you forty for it."

He shook his head. "I'm sorry, but I very much want a Rafferty."

"My wife had her heart set on it." The woman tried to look appropriately downcast, but her hard features looked more angry than sad.

"I'm sorry, madam," the older man replied. "But there is no room for negotiation."

The man in shorts got very red in the face. For a moment I thought he was going to strike the older man. Then his wife reached out and touched his arm. He took a deep breath.

"You'll be sorry," he said in a fierce whisper. Turning around, he and his wife marched out of the gallery.

"I'm sorry that happened," I said to the older man.

He smiled. "They did seem to want it very badly, didn't they? You were very brave and altruistic to award the painting to me."

I shrugged. "I meant what I said. We had already agreed, at least implicitly. Plus I don't like pushy people."

The man nodded his head. "Yes, he was certainly no gentleman."

We walked over to the desk where I indicated that he could sit to write out his check. While he was doing that, I glanced over at Miranda and Harold. Harold was rooted to the spot, his eyes in a fixed stare, as if he had just witnessed a horrific accident, which I'm sure was exactly how he felt at seeing a painting sell for over twenty times more than one of his own. Miranda watched him anxiously.

"Would you like a glass of water?" she asked. At the almost imperceptible nod of his head, she rushed to the washroom in the back of the gallery.

"My name is Arthur Peabody," the man said, handing me his check.

"Laura Magee." I reached out and took his check, and we shook hands.

"I'd like to ask a favor of you," he said in a lowered voice.

I looked to see that the amount on the check was correct.

"Of course," I said, always willing to accommodate a customer who paid in full.

"I'm staying in a bed-and-breakfast, and I don't really have anywhere to secure the painting. The staff comes in daily to clean my room, and I wouldn't want the painting just lying about. I was wondering if you'd be willing to keep it here for a few days until I'm ready to leave town."

"Sure, we'll keep it right in the back."

The man reached over and touched my shoulder, indicating that I should lean closer. As I bent toward him I caught the smell of woodsy aftershave and wool.

"It's possible that I won't be able to claim the painting in person," he whispered. "Circumstances may intervene. If that should happen, a surrogate will call for it."

I paused, thinking about legal ramifications. "How will I know that this person is authorized to act in your name? Do you have a cell phone number where you can be reached?"

"No." Mr. Peabody thought for a moment, then his voice dropped even lower. "He will say the word 'starfish.' Then you will know he is legitimate."

I paused. "Okay."

"Let this be our secret," he said, squeezing my arm.

I nodded.

He got to his feet then shook hands with me again.

"It has been a pleasure doing business with you."

"The pleasure was all mine," I replied.

He took another long look at the Rafferty, then walked out of the gallery.

I went over to Miranda and Harold. He was sipping water and appeared to have regained the use of his limbs, although his head was shaking back and forth as if trying to deny what had just happened.

"I don't get it," he said hoarsely. "Why would anyone pay twenty thousand for that?"

"The art market doesn't make any sense, dear. It just is what it is," said Miranda.

"What has this guy Rafferty got that I don't have?" he asked plaintively.

I almost said "talent" but bit it back just in time. Instead, I walked over to the Rafferty, looked again at the two little arrows, and smiled.

"Was it okay that I didn't let the sale turn into an auction?" I asked Miranda.

She nodded. "I didn't like the looks of those two anyway. Their check might bounce."

"But the picture could have sold for even more."

Miranda gave Harold a sideways glance. "Just as well it didn't," she replied.

CHAPTER 3

After several more glasses of water and many soothing words from Miranda, Harold finally left the gallery, ready, no doubt, to portray more seabirds in acrylic. I generously offered to give Miranda my commission on the Rafferty, since it had been technically her turn to wait on a customer. However, she graciously pointed out that we had agreed to let me handle sales of abstract art. After much strained politeness on both sides, we agreed that I'd give her a quarter of my commission, which made this the most productive day I'd had so far.

We hung out together in the gallery together until noon, when I went for lunch. I would come back to cover the one-to-four shift in the afternoon, then Miranda would do the four-to-seven.

I walked half a block along the pedestrian mall to Shore Mementos, the tourist shop where my new friend Angie Tortelli worked. We'd first met about two weeks ago when I ate my lunch at a bench right outside her shop, and we got to chatting. Angie was a few years younger than I am, but we had enough in common to enjoy having lunch together. Today I told her about my first big sale. All I left out was any mention of starfish. Somehow the earnest way that Mr. Peabody had insisted it be a secret made me reluctant to tell anyone.

Angie sighed. "I wish I sold on commission. Then I'd be more motivated to do my job."

"Your salary is better than mine. Most days I just take home the minimum wage."

"Still, it would be nice to have some incentive to work."

Angie took a big bite of her tuna on a roll, while I forked up more of my salad. Angie had a pretty face, but was carrying about twenty extra pounds. I knew her well enough to guess she tried to drown her unhappiness with work and with her life in general by eating. But today she seemed more restless than usual, as though she had something big to tell me.

"I wasn't going to say anything because I'm not sure whether it will happen," she finally began.

"What will happen?"

"I met this guy yesterday."

I'd heard enough about Angie's past to know there usually was a guy lurking somewhere, like a dark cloud. Usually the kind of guy your mother would have warned you to stay away from. Not that her previous boyfriends were all convicted felons, but most of them had at least come close to a tussle with the law. Although we'd only known each other for two weeks, I was already seeing her as a younger sister, so I was ready to be protective.

"What guy?" I asked a little more sharply than I intended.

"His name is Stephen Anders. He seems nice," Angie said with a note of surprise in her voice, as if she couldn't believe a nice guy would be interested in her. "He's pretty good-looking."

"How did you meet him?" I asked, ready to hear she'd met him in a bar.

"He came into the store yesterday afternoon. He said that he'd seen us eating outside yesterday and decided he wanted to get to know me better."

I felt an ugly wave of jealousy. He'd had a choice between the two of us and had picked Angie over sleek, trim me.

"What have you found out about him?"

"He's a school teacher in Philadelphia. Once the weather gets nice, he comes out whenever he can, and he likes to spend most of the summer here."

"How old is he?"

"A little old. I'd guess he's close to thirty."

"Do you know anything about his family?"

"He's got a brother and his parents." Angie paused and took a breath. "Jeez, Laura, lighten up. I only had a few minutes to talk to him. I wasn't able to conduct a full interrogation."

I smiled. "Sorry. I guess I get a little nervous when some guy just appears out of nowhere."

Angie smiled back. "So do I. Don't worry, I'll be careful."

We worked on our lunches for a few minutes in silence, watching the midday crowds walk past us in a slow but steady trickle. They stared in the store windows, pointed things out to each other, and either went inside or not depending on whether the display caught their interest. I even saw a couple go into the art gallery and hoped Miranda would make a sale.

"I've been wondering whether you'd like me to keep my eyes open for somebody for you," Angie began tentatively. "I know you've been seeing that cop back home, but you made it sound like it wasn't exactly a going-steady kind of thing."

Ah, yes, Detective Farantello and me. He was divorced from his wife, but his teenage daughter, who had diabetes, always seemed to be guilt-tripping them into getting back together again. That would last until they realized why they had gotten divorced in the first place, after which he would come back to me. When I'd left home a few weeks ago, his daughter was having another crisis, and he had gone back to his wife after we'd spent the winter seeing each other regularly. I'd about had my fill of his migratory patterns.

"If anyone should happen along, I'd be willing to take a look," I said cautiously. Angie, being only twenty-two to my twenty-eight, ran with a younger crowd. "I don't want to start dating

19

college guys or high school graduates working as plumber's assistants."

Angie nodded solemnly then grinned. "Wouldn't it be great, though? Maybe we could double-date."

I nodded noncommittally. Double dating with a twenty-two-year-old would certainly make me feel old, especially since my twenty-ninth birthday was next month. The very thought made my stomach lurch, because after that came the dreaded thirty. Then you weren't a young person anymore, and should be well set on your course in life. Or so they said, whoever *they* were. Somehow I didn't think working as an advice columnist for a small paper and spending the summers as a sales clerk in an art gallery constituted a solid long-term plan. Most of my friends had gotten married by now, some of them more than once, and a few of them had even started families. I hadn't even found a career yet. Maybe I did deserve to be hanging out with people almost ten years younger than I, since that was about my maturity level.

"What's the matter?" Angie asked.

"What do you mean?"

"You suddenly got this really worried expression."

"That's my usual expression."

Angie laughed. I packed up my garbage and checked my watch. It was almost time for me to relieve Miranda.

"Do you want to do something tonight?" I asked.

"I'll let you know later. Stephen said he might call, so I have to keep my evening open for him."

"Don't worry about it," I said. "Anyway, I need to go out for a run after work and then spend some time cleaning my apartment. How about tomorrow?"

"That will be great, if I'm free."

I hoped she wasn't putting too much stock in this Stephen guy.

As I walked back down the mall heading to work, I began to feel sorry for myself. Poor little Cinderella would spend the evening cleaning, while lucky Angie got to go out with the prince. I wondered what my chances were of finding a fairy godmother, and decided they weren't good. If I wanted my love life to improve, I'd have to be my own fairy godmother.

CHAPTER 4

When I got back to the store I met a happy and relieved Miranda, who had just completed wrapping Harold's painting of the right-facing seagull he had been stressing about in the morning.

I studied the couple as they handed Miranda their credit card. They were both well dressed in a preppie sort of way and glancing at each other smugly, as if they had just made a terrific deal. It was certainly a large painting, so if you figured how much you paid per square inch, nine hundred dollars might seem a reasonable price. But I figured that unless you happened to have an empty spot over a sectional in a room that you were decorating in shoreline chic, Harold's work was expensive at half the price. The couple left the gallery whispering nervously, as if afraid that Miranda would recognize her error at selling them the painting at such a low price and attempt to take it back.

"Harold will be delighted to hear that we sold the gull," she said, excitement and relief mixed in her tone. "We're going out to dinner tonight, and I wasn't looking forward to spending the entire evening trying to bolster his ego after that Rafferty sold. At least now he has a sale of his own."

"I was pretty surprised myself we sold a painting for that much money."

"It doesn't happen often, but Mr. Tompkins advertises in art magazines and in newspapers in Philadelphia and New York. I think he's pretty well known in the art world. So when collectors come down here for a vacation, they often stop in to see what he's got. We never carry more than five or six of those modern paintings, but when they sell, you make a good commission."

Miranda went in the back room. When she returned she had her handbag in one hand and her car keys in the other.

"I'll be back at four. See if you can sell another twenty-thousand dollar painting by then."

"Give me a few days and Tompkins will have to get more inventory."

Miranda laughed and headed out the door.

The worst part of this job was the hours spent alone. There just wasn't anything to do once you had carefully dusted the paintings and vacuumed the carpet. The phone never seemed to ring unless it was a friend of Miranda's looking for her. When customers came through the door I would pounce on them like a hungry lioness, trying to keep the conversation going as long as possible to perk up my day.

Finally, I had taken to reading while on the job. And because we had to be dressed formally, I also got tired of standing in high heels, so now I sat down behind our desk on the showroom floor and read. I confined myself to books about art, so if Mr. Tompkins should come in and catch me, I could claim my reading was job related.

I was currently working my way through a book on contemporary sculpture and was holding the book at arm's length, studying what looked like a rhinoceros horn covered in aluminum paint, when I happened to glance toward the front of the store and saw a man staring in at me. He caught my eye and grinned. A second later the bell jingled as he walked in the store.

"Reading glasses might help with that," he said and smiled.

His smile was infectious and I smiled back.

"I don't think glasses would do any good," I said, showing him the picture.

"I see what you mean." He gave a helpless shrug. "Who knows with modern art?"

"Not all modern art is like that," I said. "Come over here and take a look at this."

I walked over to the contemporary art side of the room, motioning for him to follow me. I pointed to a small painting hanging in the corner where it was easily obscured by its larger neighbors. The canvas was covered with blotches of paint, a sort of tiny Jackson Pollock lookalike. But it had a completeness and unity that appealed to me.

The man studied it for a long moment, which gave me a chance to give him the onceover. He was around six feet tall with a full head of tousled brown hair that hadn't seen a comb recently. His jeans were worn and his denim work shirt was a roadmap of wrinkles. But none of this served to obscure the fact that he was handsome.

Finally, his blue eyes left the canvas and rested on me.

"What do you like about it?"

I paused. "The way the artist knew exactly when to stop."

"Maybe he just ran out of paint," the man said, but with a smile that softened the remark.

"No. I think he had a concept of the kind of balance he wanted, and was sure when he achieved it."

"Maybe you're right," he said. "But what about that one?"

He pointed to a painting of trees that reminded me of Hockney. Someone named T.J. Rasmussen had painted it. The finely drawn details were very realistic, making the trees appear as if they were etched out of paint, but the lavenders and blues were almost surrealistic.

"Isn't that one great?" I said.

"I'll take it," he announced.

"Excuse me?" I said, thinking I'd misheard him. When it came to art, people hemmed and hawed even more than when buying a car. Now, in one day, I'd had two customers come in and make immediate choices, and they were selections of modern art.

"I'd like to buy it," he repeated slowly, as if afraid that I might have a hearing or learning deficiency. "The slip on it says two thousand dollars. Is that right?"

"That's what it says," I responded, expecting him to haggle over the price.

"Okay."

"Are you sure?" I asked, still filled with disbelief.

"Positive."

I took the painting down and carried it into the packing area. The man followed along behind me. Realizing I still didn't know his name, I stuck out my hand and said, "I'm Laura Magee."

He took my hand in his. His hand was large with carefully trimmed fingernails.

"I'm Mike Rogers."

He looked in the direction of where the Rafferty was leaning against the wall.

"That's an interesting picture."

"I'm afraid it just sold today."

"Probably to some hip young couple."

"No, actually to an older gentleman with a very discerning eye."

"Ah, contemporary art isn't just for the young."

"We're holding it here for him until he's ready to leave town."

"I see."

"Will you be paying with a check or credit card?" I asked.

His face became thoughtful. "Could I give you a cash deposit, then pay the rest of it when I come in to pick it up?"

"I can hold a painting for a week with a ten percent deposit."

Mike took out his wallet and pulled out four fifties. I filled out a receipt slip and handed it to him.

"I'm surprised you carry so much modern and contemporary stuff here," Mike said, glancing around the gallery. "I would have thought only *that* stuff would be good sellers," he said, pointing to one of Harold's bird portraits.

"We do sell a lot of nature paintings, of course, but a lot of folks come here from Philadelphia and New York to vacation. And this gallery has a surprisingly wide reputation," I said, repeating the answer I'd gotten from Miranda.

He nodded. "I was wondering, would you be free to go out to dinner with me tomorrow night?"

I'm pretty much free for dinner every night, I thought. I didn't say it because that would make me sound truly pathetic. But then I recalled the wise older sister advice I'd been giving Angie about not going out with people she didn't know.

"You didn't buy this picture just so I would go out with you, did you?" I asked.

He gave me one of his brilliant smiles.

"Do you think a date with you is worth two thousand dollars?"

"Strictly speaking, you've only paid two hundred."

He laughed. "Fair enough."

"I just want you to know that I don't go out with customers as a reward for buying a painting."

"Okay. But is there some unwritten rule in the ethics of art dealing saying that you can't go out with a customer?"

"Not that I know of, but I'm naturally a bit cautious about going out with men I don't know."

He spread his arms wide as if inviting me to pat him down. The thought was attractive.

"Ask me anything you want. I'm an open book."

I shook my head. "I'll go out with you and ask my questions then. How about we meet at the Union Restaurant on Prescott? Do you know where it is?"

"I can find it. Are you sure you don't want me to pick you up?"

"I'm sure." I wasn't going to let a guy know where I lived on our first date.

"Seven o'clock."

"Better make it closer to seven-twenty. I have to work until seven that night."

He nodded and smiled. "And don't let anyone get their hands on that painting," he said, waving in the general direction of the one he'd selected and the Rafferty.

"They'll be safe here," I promised.

A concerned expression passed over his face, then he said he was looking forward to our date and left.

I leaned back against the desk and tried to absorb the events of the day. Miraculously I'd sold two pieces of contemporary art in one day, when normally I'd be lucky to sell one a month. And on top of that, a handsome stranger had asked me out, which surprised me even more. But it also concerned me. My track record with men hasn't been so good that I can go along blithely assuming the best. Back home in a small city it was easy to check on people, but here in a tourist town there would be folks floating through all the time. You had to be more careful. All I really knew about Mike was that he could apparently afford to purchase a two-thousand-dollar painting without giving it a lot of thought. But as he had admitted himself, so far he'd only invested two hundred. For someone in my tax bracket that was still pretty impressive, but he could be an operator. Be alert, I warned myself. Don't be taken in by a handsome face.

I just hoped I'd listen to my own good advice.

CHAPTER 5

Miranda had been pretty impressed, almost to the point of envy, when I told her about selling the Rasmussen. But I was thinking more about Mike. I thought about Mike as I walked back to my condo. I continued thinking about him as I scrubbed the bathroom from top to bottom then went on to vacuum the sea-foam green carpeting that extended throughout the house except for the kitchen and bathroom.

Although my grandmother, who has been heavily influenced by her own eccentric readings of Taoism, would have warned me that I should think about the task at hand and do what I am doing, I found thinking about Mike and speculating on our first date to be much pleasanter than focusing on the cleaning of the toilet or the mopping of the floor. But I did find that after almost two straight hours of mining what little information I had about him, the subject of Mike had become a bit stale. I ended up wondering whether wanting my apartment so neat and orderly was a sign of encroaching spinsterhood.

Fortunately the topic of Mike ran dry at about the time I was ready for my run. Right across the street from my place was a boardwalk that went from one end of Safe Harbor Beach to the other. I was at just about the southern end, and a run from there to the other end was two miles. I ran the first two miles at a fairly leisurely pace, but then tried to challenge myself a bit more on the return. Back in Massachusetts I'd done aerobics on an elliptical trainer and walking on a treadmill, but I'd quickly found that nothing got me in the same shape as running did. As long as my knees could take it, I planned to continue, even after I returned home, although running there would be nothing like running next to the beach.

As I ran, I found myself thinking about what I would do when the summer was over. A part of me wanted to return to my grandmother's and resume work as Auntie Mabel on the *Ravensford Chronicle*. But another part of me wanted to go back to Boston and see if I could find a job there. Maybe I could freelance on *Picture This!,* an underground art magazine I'd worked on while moonlighting from the museum. Reality stepped in, however, and warned me that I'd never make enough money that way to afford even a fraction of a Boston apartment.

I could always live with Mom and Dad, I told myself, and felt my stomach tighten into knots. They'd be happy to have me, but in a few weeks I'd be enrolled in a teachers' education program somewhere. My mother, a teacher, always said I should get my teaching certificate so I'd have something to fall back on, and I knew she thought I had definitely fallen. Spending the rest of my life as a teacher conjured up year after year of drudgery broken up by the periodic oases of summer vacations. What a monotonous life!

As if to prove I didn't have to be a creature of habit, I took the next ramp off the boardwalk and decided to finish my run by going through town. I was going down Presidents' Street, which is one of the main drags and lined with bed and breakfasts, when I saw him come down the walk from Elizabeth's Inn. It was Arthur Peabody. I stopped in my tracks as he turned away from me and headed in the other direction. He hadn't seen me. The polite thing to do would have been to cross over to the other side of the street and keep running, or perhaps to have caught up to him and said hello. I didn't do either of those polite things. Instead, I slowed to a walk and began to follow him.

Now I have to admit that this isn't the first time I've followed someone. Occasionally, when living in Boston, I'd spot an acquaintance before he or she saw me, and I would follow whoever it was, being careful not to be spotted. Why would I take such a risk of social embarrassment? I'm not absolutely certain, but I know I get a thrill at being able to observe someone when they don't know they're being watched. Not that I'm a Peeping Tom who wants to spy on people getting undressed in their bedrooms. I'm much more interested in following them as they go through their normal daily routine. To make it all sound a bit nicer than it is, I'm really curious about how other people live their lives when they think they are unobserved.

Mr. Peabody was easy to follow. He headed straight down Presidents' Street, going at a good clip for an older guy. I followed along, feeling the unpleasant sensation of sweat drying on my body. He crossed at Madison and went one block over. Now he was right behind the pedestrian mall. I could see the back of the art gallery from where I was standing. He went right past the end of the mall and paused at Union Street, probably the busiest traffic spot in town. He carefully looked both ways and began to cross.

He had just stepped off the curb when a black SUV drove past me and made a sharp right, pausing until Peabody had reached the middle of the street. Then it suddenly sped up. There was a thud of impact and Peabody was thrown in the air like a giant rag doll, arms and legs in disarray. The SUV raced away. Someone screamed, and I started running toward where he had landed.

Peabody lay on his back with blood running over his face. I took one of his hands in mine. His eyes stayed closed.

"Somebody call nine-one-one!" I shouted, hearing an edge of hysteria in my voice.

Peabody's eyes opened. They were unfocused at first, but then they fixed on me and he smiled in recognition.

"Remember, wait for starfish," he said. Then his eyes closed.

CHAPTER 6

I had never seen anyone die before. But from what I've heard from others who have, Mr. Peabody's leaving was more peaceful than most. He just closed his eyes and died. I like to think that as a dignified man, he would have been happy to know he left this life with proper decorum. But even a neat, clean leaving of life can be pretty upsetting to the ones left behind, and although I can't say that I knew him well, I knew him well enough that I sat on the curb feeling stunned until the detectives came for me.

There were two of them. One of the police officers in uniform who had talked to me had already pointed them in my direction. The man was tall and almost painfully thin; the woman was short and stocky. Neither one of them looked the least bit sympathetic as they came sauntering toward me as if they owned the world. I stood up, hoping that would help put us on equal terms. Fortunately, my knees didn't wobble, although I was feeling stiff after my run.

They introduced themselves. Detective Belsen was the woman and Detective Joiner was the guy.

"You're Laura Magee?" Detective Belsen asked, giving me an accusatory look as if she expected me to deny it.

"That's right."

"And you knew the deceased."

I nodded.

"How did you come to know him?"

I explained about how Mr. Peabody had come into the gallery and purchased a painting.

"So he bought the painting then left it with you?" Detective Joiner asked.

"That's right."

"Did he pay a lot for it?"

"Twenty thousand."

The two detectives looked at each other as if that was a lot of money.

"That's a pretty pricey painting," the male detective said. "Who painted it?"

"Rafferty," I said.

"Never heard of him."

"I think he's contemporary."

Joiner raised an eyebrow.

"He's still alive," I explained.

He nodded. "Yeah, I guess only the dead ones are famous."

I looked across the street. The crowd had dispersed quickly when the uniformed officers urged them to move along. Probably no one was anxious to ruin their vacation by viewing a dead body. By now Mr. Peabody's body had been loaded into an ambulance and taken away. In a few minutes there would be no sign of the tragedy that had happened here.

Detective Belsen cleared her throat to get my attention.

"I understand how you met the deceased. What I don't understand is how you happened to be on the scene when he got hit by the SUV."

I tried to think of a good way to put it, but nothing came to mind.

"I was following him."

Detective Belsen's eyes bored into mine.

"Why were you following him?"

"Well, I was out for my evening run," I said, glancing down

at my t-shirt and shorts as if providing proof. "And I happened to see Mr. Peabody come out of an inn. So I just followed him."

"In other words, you were stalking him?" Belsen said.

I sighed. "Don't you ever see someone you know and follow them just to find out where they're going?"

"Not unless I'm on the job," the woman said. "Are you sure you weren't working with the folks in the SUV to keep an eye on him?"

"Yeah, that's why I stayed around to wait for you after he died."

Belsen looked like she wanted to respond to that, but her partner butted in.

"Did you notice that the SUV was following him?"

"It was behind me. I didn't see it at all until the last minute."

"That's what you're telling us, anyway," Detective Belsen said.

"It's the truth," I replied, knowing that sounded pretty weak.

Belsen asked, "Did you see a plate? Get a number?"

"No." I felt silly.

"Could it have just been an accident?" Joiner asked.

I shook my head. "He was in the middle of the road. The driver had plenty of time to see him. It sure looked intentional to me."

Joiner asked me for my address and phone number. He made it pretty clear that they might be contacting me in the future, so I should "make myself available," which I figured was a fancy way of telling me not to leave town. They were just about to turn away and leave when a thought occurred to me.

"What should I do with Mr. Peabody's painting?" I asked.

"He's already paid for it, right?" Joiner said.

I nodded.

"Then it's part of his estate. When we contact his next of kin, we'll try to find out who the executor of his estate is and let that person know about the painting. Just hang onto it until then," Joiner said.

I watched them walk away, heading toward their nondescript sedan. Suddenly, it came to me about starfish. I almost called out to them, but then decided that starfish could stay a secret between Mr. Peabody and me, since I wasn't too thrilled with the way Detective Belsen had treated me. But what would I do with the painting if someone came into the gallery and whispered "starfish" in my ear? Would I give it to him or her or hold onto it for the estate? I decided that was a problem I'd work on once it arose.

CHAPTER 7

The next morning I woke up feeling stiffer than usual, and when I remembered about Mr. Peabody's death, my mind felt even worse than my body. I'd come home from talking to the police, had a little supper and spent the rest of the evening sprawled in front of the television not really paying attention to what was on the screen. My mind kept replaying the moment when Mr. Peabody had smiled at me, then died. Even when I finally fell into an exhausted sleep many hours later, I woke up at around three with the same image in my mind. I tossed and turned and dozed for a few more hours until I decided I might as well start the day and got up.

I took a long shower to loosen my tight muscles, then had a bowl of cereal along with two cups of strong coffee to jumpstart my foggy mind. I had to get myself in some kind of presentable shape for work. So I dressed with unusual care, and was pleased to be greeted by a cool and not humid June morning. After walking the six blocks to work, I still felt unwilted. Miranda was already in the gallery.

"One of our local artists is bringing in a couple of pieces this morning, and I wanted to be here to price them."

I heard a noise in the back, and Harold wandered out holding a cup of coffee in one hand and vigorously scratching his beard with the other. It made my face itch to watch him. I nodded hello and got a salute with his coffee cup in return.

"Harold wanted to be here to scope out the local competition," Miranda whispered in my ear.

I knew there was a local artists' association made up of twenty or so intensely competitive local painters who supplied most of the nature paintings to the six picture galleries in town. They were constantly checking out each other's work to discover what was selling and if anyone had come up with a new angle on the old subjects.

"I just don't see it," Harold growled from the back room.

"Here we go again," Miranda muttered. "He's looking at the Rafferty."

Harold wandered out and stared at each of us as if searching for agreement.

"Don't see what, Harold?" I asked with deep reluctance.

"I don't see how anyone would pay twenty thousand dollars for a painting that doesn't mean anything."

He turned and wandered into the back room again to take another look. Apparently the painting horrified and fascinated him in equal measure.

"When is Mr. Peabody going to get that painting out of here?" Miranda whispered. "It's getting to be all that Harold wants to talk about."

"Well there's been a hitch in the plans there," I said, and went on to tell her about Mr. Peabody's death.

Her eyes grew wide by the middle of my story, and when I reached the end she was wiping away tears.

"Oh, my God! It's all my fault," she said.

"What do you mean?"

"That couple that was here when Mr. Peabody bought the painting, they came back yesterday at around five. They wanted to know Mr. Peabody's address in town."

"Why?"

"They said they wanted to make him another offer on the painting. I should never have given out that information,"

Miranda said. "But I thought I was doing a good thing. It was a chance for Mr. Peabody to make more money."

"We don't know that they were the ones who hit Mr. Peabody," I said.

"But you saw how angry that man was when Mr. Peabody got the painting."

"It's only a possibility, but you should call the police and let them know."

I gave her the names of the detectives.

"And now we can't get rid of this painting until the executor of his will shows up," Miranda said, twisting her hands nervously, having apparently recovered from her guilt rather quickly, and returning to the problem of Harold. "Who knows when that will be? It might take months. I can't put up with Harold being this way for another couple of days, let alone a couple of months. What are we going to do?"

"I guess we try to find someplace else to store the painting. Why don't you see if Mr. Tompkins has any ideas?"

"I can't do that. He'd want to know why I didn't want to keep it here at the gallery. I couldn't tell him about Harold. Mr. Tompkins has only met Harold once, and they didn't really get along. They have differing views of art."

With Mr. Tompkins's good eye for contemporary work, I wasn't surprised.

"Why don't you take it home with you?" Miranda said.

"You want me to take home a twenty-thousand-dollar work of art?"

"Just for a little while. I'll ask Mr. Tompkins to get in touch with his lawyer to see if he can find out who Mr. Peabody's executor might be."

I shook my head. "My condo isn't that secure."

"It's as secure as the gallery. Maybe even more secure. Nobody is going to think that you have a valuable work of art hanging on your wall. They'll assume it's just a cheap piece of sofa art. Nobody will think twice about it."

I was about to shake my head again when Harold wandered back, gesticulating to himself.

"Please, will you just do it for me," Miranda asked.

I couldn't say no.

Miranda thanked me effusively then went into the back room to call the police. The door opened and a woman came in carrying a painting under each arm.

She leaned one of the paintings against my desk and stuck out her hand. "Hi, I'm Corey Lanier." I shook her hand and asked to see her work. Harold picked that moment to wander out from the back again.

"Corey," he said with a brief nod.

"Harold," she replied.

I pulled out an easel for her to put her paintings on. She lifted the first one into place. It showed a dramatically high dune with the surf pounding into shore in the background.

"Very nice," I said and meant it. Although I was heartily sick of seaside paintings, she showed a nice use of color and composition.

"Where is that dune?" Harold asked suspiciously.

"I based it on the one at North Beach."

Harold shook his head. "That dune is nowhere near as high as you show it there."

"I made it higher to give more drama to the scene."

"You mean you exaggerated what was there."

"I see nothing wrong in that. I'm a painter, not a photographer."

"You mean you're a liar. You're telling people there's a dune like that when there really isn't."

Corey turned bright red. She leaned toward Harold.

"That's called creativity. Something you wouldn't know

39

anything about."

It was Harold's turn to go red from his forehead to the beginning of his beard.

"I believe in honesty," he said. "In showing nature as it actually is. Not in making up some phony scene. What are you going to do next? A picture of elephants walking on the beach?"

"This is what I *did* next." She put the second picture up on the easel. It was a heartbreakingly beautiful picture of sunrise over the ocean.

"That's wonderful," I said.

Harold stood there chewing on his lower lip.

"Aren't you going to tell me that sunrise never looks that good?" Corey challenged.

He turned and walked into the back room.

"Harold has good technique, but no imagination," Corey said softly to me.

Miranda came out of the back. "What's the matter with—oh, hi, Corey."

"Hi, Miranda."

"What have you brought for us today?"

Corey showed her two pieces and Miranda sounded properly appreciative. She promised to have them out on the floor by the afternoon.

"I'm sorry if I upset Harold," Corey said as she prepared to leave.

"Don't worry about it," Miranda said. "He's kind of sensitive. It's that artistic temperament, you know."

Corey nodded, managing to keep a deadpan expression.

When she left the store, Miranda turned to me.

"I talked to a Detective Joiner. He wants me to come down to the station to answer a few questions."

"Well, don't let them rattle you, especially his partner Detective Belsen. She'll try to make you feel guilty."

"I already do," Miranda said, looking truly miserable.

"You didn't run down Mr. Peabody."

"But I should never have given out his personal information without contacting him first."

"He didn't give us a cell phone number, so how could you have contacted him?"

"I know. I just can't help feeling at least partly responsible."

Miranda walked into the back room and returned with her handbag.

"They wanted to see you right away?" I asked.

"I had the feeling that if I didn't show up within an hour, they'd be down here."

"Did Harold leave?" The last thing I wanted was to have Harold hanging around in his depressed state.

She nodded. "He slipped out the back. I guess he didn't want to see Corey again. Sometimes he's just too competitive for his own good. I wish he could relax more, but painting is his life."

"I guess it is."

"Well, I'll be going."

"Good luck," I called to her as she went out the door. If she ended up dealing with Detective Belsen, she'd probably need it.

Chapter 8

I was sitting at the desk reading a book about Renaissance art when a man walked into the gallery. Something about him looked familiar, but it took a minute before it clicked. I jumped to my feet, dropping the book on the floor.

"Good morning, Mr. Tompkins," I stammered.

You might think I'd remember what the owner of the gallery looked like, but I had only met him briefly two weeks before and frankly, he hadn't made much of an impression. He was tall and thin with a head that protruded forward from shoulders rounded in a buzzard-like way. We had exchanged a few general pleasantries and shared a story about the person at the Museum of Fine Arts who had recommended me. But our conversation had all been rather unfocused. There had been no discussion of my responsibilities or his expectations for my performance. All of that was left to Miranda. He seemed satisfied just to have seen me and found me not to have two heads or an indecipherable accent.

Today he gave me another of his vague smiles and looked around the gallery with the bewildered expression of someone who had never seen it before.

"You dropped something," he said, pointing at the book.

I bent down and scooped it up. I waited for him to say something about my reading on the job, but he continued to look carefully about him as if trying to commit everything to memory. Finally, he cleared his throat. I readied myself to hear what he had to say, but it was several seconds before he began.

"I heard that you had sold a Rafferty, and I wanted to take another look at it."

I nodded and got ready to lead him into the back room, but he continued speaking.

"Miranda sends me an e-mail every evening detailing what's been sold that day. I was very surprised to hear that the Rafferty had sold so fast."

It was my turn to clear my throat.

"Well, there's been a bit of a problem with that sale," I said, and then went on to tell him about the events of last evening.

If I had expected him to look shocked, I was sorely disappointed. He did raise his eyebrows a couple of times and say "Oh, really" and "Yes," but generally he absorbed the information with as much reaction as if I had been reciting our sales list for the week.

"It's unusual for us to have a patron die so suddenly," he finally announced in a matter-of-fact way.

I didn't know what to say to that, so I just nodded.

"That means we still have the Rafferty, correct?"

"Until the executor of Mr. Peabody's estate claims it. Miranda thought that your lawyer might be able to find out more about that."

"Yes, yes, I'll ask around and see. May I take a look at the painting?"

"Of course," I said, and led him into the back room.

He stood in front of the Rafferty, his eyes roaming around the picture as if absorbing every detail. He made a dry coughing sound when he spotted the two arrows. I decided that what I'd heard was a laugh.

"That's a pretty neat trick, putting in those arrows," I said. "A real comment on modern art."

"Indeed," Tompkins replied, cutting off my enthusiasm. He

reached out as if to touch the painting, then drew his hand back.

"Perhaps we will be able to buy this back from the executor of Peabody's estate. You said that couple who was here was willing to pay more than what we sold it for, which means others may be willing to do so as well."

I nodded, not sure what the odds were of selling the Rafferty twice.

Seeming to read my mind, he said, "It only takes one person."

"You're right. In fact, we sold the Rasmussen yesterday," I said, pointing to the picture.

"Oh, to whom?"

When I told him, Mr. Tompkins shook his head. "Not a name I recognize. Make sure you get him on our mailing list."

"Of course."

"Why isn't Miranda here?" he asked, looking about him as if noticing her absence for the first time. "She should be here checking in new works."

"She had to go talk to the police about Mr. Peabody's death."

"Why is that?"

I explained Miranda's involvement in the whole thing, trying to make her appear as innocent as possible.

He listened to what I said expressionlessly, then nodded.

"Most unfortunate. But I'm sure the police cannot possibly hold her responsible for such a normal mistake. After all, we don't expect the people we come across in daily life to be criminals, do we?"

"I suppose not," I replied, although that husband and wife team had definitely seemed a bit suspicious.

"Anyway, it could have been a perfectly normal hit-and-run. With the way people drive, we're lucky there aren't more of them in Safe Harbor. People think any unusual death is a murder these days. Comes from watching too much television."

Mr. Tompkins began walking back to the front of the shop. He stopped for a moment and stared at one of Harold's seascapes. He shook his head sadly.

"It's amazing how much of this kind of thing we sell. Everyone who owns a house or condo anywhere near the beach seems to feel compelled to decorate with a seaside theme." He sighed. "But I guess I shouldn't complain. If we didn't sell a lot of these, we wouldn't be able to stay in business and sell the occasional Rafferty."

I didn't respond, not wanting to say anything negative about Harold that might get repeated to Miranda.

Suddenly, Mr. Tompkins turned and stared at me closely.

"Congratulations, Ms. Magee, on your two sales of contemporary art in the same week. I'm sure that's a record. But don't let your success cause you to develop an unrealistic set of expectations. You may not sell another piece of it for a month. Fortunately, the sales of these other things," he said, waving a dismissive hand in the direction of the seascapes, "will provide you with what I hope will be adequate commissions."

"I'll keep that in mind."

"And let Miranda know I was here." He frowned as if still a bit annoyed by her absence. "Tell her I hope her experience with the police was not too unpleasant."

Giving me a brief nod, he took one final survey of the gallery then sailed out of the store.

CHAPTER 9

At eleven forty-five the door opened and Miranda came into the gallery. She spread her arms wide and collapsed into a chair.

"It was terrible. They treated me like I was a criminal, especially that Belsen woman. How was I supposed to know those two were going to run down poor Mr. Peabody?"

"Are the police sure they did it?"

"Pretty much. Apparently a witness got a look into the SUV, and said there was a couple fitting their description in the front seat."

"That doesn't prove it was the same couple."

"It was. About fifteen minutes after the accident, they showed up at the inn where Peabody was staying, claiming to be his son and daughter-in-law. They wanted to be let into his room to get some medicine he needed. The innkeeper said he would go up with them. I guess to make certain that was all they took."

"What happened?"

"The three of them went up to the room. They weren't able to find the medicine, and they left."

"They were looking to see if the painting was there."

"I suppose."

"I wonder what's so special about that Rafferty."

Miranda shrugged. "Those detectives kept saying that I should be more protective of my customers' privacy, like I purposely set him up to be killed. They even suggested that I might have been in on it. I can't believe that we pay the salaries of these people, and they treat us this way."

"I suppose they spend so much time dealing with criminals, they start to think everyone is like that."

"Don't make excuses for them," Miranda snapped. She put her hands on her temples and pressed. "Sorry, but all this has given me a raging headache."

"Would you like to go home? I can take over for the afternoon if you'll give me a few minutes to run out and buy some lunch."

Miranda smiled. "Thanks. But when I'm feeling this miserable, I may as well be at work. If I go home, I'll just fuss and fume and not get anything worthwhile done."

"Mr. Tompkins came into the gallery today."

"And I wasn't here," Miranda said, almost breaking into a wail. "Can this day get any better?"

"I told him you were with the police."

"That wouldn't make any difference to him. Tompkins is a man of set habits. He would expect me to be here pricing the new artworks that I haven't even unpacked."

"He was surprised not to see you, but I think he understood that you had no choice."

Miranda shook her head. "He would have told me to put off the police until after my work here was completed. That's probably what I should have done."

"The police were very insistent. You didn't really have a choice."

"There's always a choice," Miranda grumbled. She looked up at the clock. "It's afternoon. You should go get some lunch. I'll be fine here rehearsing what I should have said to those cops this morning."

"Are you sure?"

"Positive. Get going."

I went out into the mall. A block away I could see Angie sitting on a bench, already eating her lunch. I gave her a wave and darted into my favorite sandwich shop and got a tuna on rye and lemonade.

"Sorry I'm late," I said as I settled onto the bench next to her.

"No problem."

"We've been having some difficulties with the police."

"What did you do now?" she joked. But her expression turned grim when I explained about the Peabody accident.

"Who would believe that something like that could happen here in Safe Harbor?"

"I guess nowhere is really safe."

Angie nodded and sat there with an excited smile on her face. I could tell that, as soon as I asked, information would come pouring out.

"So what's new with you?"

"I had a date with Stephen last night."

I gave her a poke in the arm. "Good for you. How did it go?"

"Great. We went to a movie then we got a custard down by the beach."

"A very traditional date."

"Yeah, not like my usual where the guy just wants to neck in the car then go to a bar where they spit on the floor."

"Sounds like Stephen is a real gentleman."

"Yeah." Her eyes looked off down the mall and got a kind of dreamy look. I figured that Angie was in the first blush of being in love.

"What did the two of you talk about?"

"Children."

"It's a little soon for that, isn't it?"

Angie giggled girlishly. "He teaches fifth grade, so we talked about his students."

"Fifth grade?"

"Yeah. A lot of men teach elementary school today," she said a trifle defensively.

"I suppose that's true."

"And some of the stories he told were really funny. You can see that he's a great teacher."

"What did you talk about?"

"Oh, my family, for one thing."

Angie came from a family with three brothers and two sisters, and there always seemed to be a lot happening, some of it funny, some of it unbelievable.

"I also talked a little bit about work. But I tried not to be too much of a downer. It's not good to whine a lot on a first date," she said as if this were some dictum she had read.

"I guess not. So are you going to see him again?"

"He drove all the way out to see me from his home. That's a two-hour trip. So I can't expect him to do that every day. But he said he'd give me a call and try to come out in a couple of days."

"A two-hour drive just to see you. That guy must have it bad," I said.

Angie blushed. "I hope so because I'm half-crazy about him already."

"Well," I said slowly, "I've met a guy myself."

Under Angie's excited questioning, I told her as much as I knew about Mike.

"He must have money to just plunk down that much cash for a painting," Angie said.

"Do you think that's important?"

"Sure it is. Guys with no money expect you to pay for everything. I've gone out with more than a few like that."

"Good point. We'll see if he pays the rest of what he owes on the painting."

"But this is great," Angie said. "Now you guys can double-date with us. How about I suggest that to Stephen the next time he calls?"

I paused to give the idea some thought.

"You can *suggest* it to Stephen, but don't make it a hard-and-fast commitment. I want to see how my first date with Mike goes before saying there will be another."

"Okay. That makes sense. But this guy sounds so great, I'm betting that there is a second date."

I gave her the patronizing smile of an older sister.

"We'll see."

After lunch I walked home and got my car. Then I drove back to the gallery. When I walked in the front door, Miranda came rushing out of the back room.

"Oh, it's only you. I thought it might be Tompkins checking up on me."

"You wanted me to bring the Rafferty home with me, so I drove my car over to transport it. If you still want me to take it, that is. What will Mr. Tompkins say if he comes by and the Rafferty is gone?"

Miranda stood there, frozen with indecision. I could see her trying to work out the possible repercussions from Mr. Tompkins for moving the work versus the certain difficulties with Harold for leaving it in the studio.

"Take it with you," she finally said. "Mr. Tompkins probably won't be coming again this week, while Harold is stopping by for a visit this afternoon. I really can't handle another session of his going on and on about the unfairness of the art world."

"Great, well, let's do it then."

We went in the back room and carefully wrapped the Rafferty for transport. I had pulled my car into a space behind the gallery, so I carried it out the back door and stowed it in the trunk of my car. Then I drove the quarter of a mile to my condo, going cautiously so as not to needlessly shift the load.

I parked in my space under the condominium and carried the picture up the set of outside stairs, and, stopping a couple of times to rest along the way, made my way to my condo on the third floor.

I went inside and surveyed my walls, looking for a likely spot to put the Rafferty. It didn't take me long to figure out that, given its size and the décor of the rooms, the best place for it was in the living room right over the sofa. Although I felt a twinge of guilt at using a twenty-thousand-dollar painting as sofa art, I quickly moved the sofa out from the wall and took down the view of the dunes that was currently hanging there. I went into the master bedroom, and by some judicious re-arranging of clothes and shoes was able to put that painting in the back of the closet. Then I hung the Rafferty on the wall, shoved the sofa into place and stood back to take a look. The painting stood out against the light coral color of the walls and really dominated the room. I knew this was a painting I could live with. In fact, I was already regretting the day when I would have to return it to the gallery.

Tearing myself away from the painting, I went into the bedroom and lay down to take a quick nap. I wanted to be at my most witty and charming tonight. Half an hour of tossing and turning told me that I was too keyed up for a nap, so I got up and took a shower and got dressed in my man-impressing clothes, since I'd be going directly from the gallery to the restaurant. I had a small bowl of yogurt to tide me over until dinner, then headed out the door.

When I walked into the gallery, Miranda was with a customer, but she glanced at me twice, so I knew I looked better than normal. She kept trying to direct the woman, who had a small child in tow, to one of Harold's tern paintings, but Corey's view of the sunset eventually won out. I knew that meant more hand-holding for Miranda once Harold discovered that Corey's newest painting had sold before one of his. Never had someone looked so unhappy to receive five hundred dollars as Miranda did.

"You look like you have some plans for after work," she said.

I nodded. "I have a date."

"Is that the first one since you've been here?"

"Yeah. The men haven't been exactly flocking around."

"Tell me about it. Wait until you hit forty, then you get all the recently divorced to pick from. And usually it's pretty obvious why they're divorced."

Since I knew Harold was divorced, I refrained from making a comment.

"What are your plans for this evening?" I asked.

Miranda shrugged. "Harold's coming over for dinner. I guess we'll watch some television or take a walk along the beach. He's looking for some new locations to spot birds."

I nodded. If I said that sounded exciting, she'd probably think I was being sarcastic, which would have been true.

"Who's the guy?" she asked.

"Actually I met him here. He's the one who bought the Rasmussen."

"Then he must have some money," she said.

I wondered if she and Angie were drinking the same water, since both seemed to put money as the highest priority in a man. Maybe that was why I always seemed to be coming up with losers.

"Is he good-looking?"

That was more the type of question I could get behind, and I described him as well as I could.

Miranda winked. "Money and good looks. Sounds like this guy is the complete package."

"We'll see."

"Take some advice from a person who's been around the

block a few more times than you have. We all start out wanting Mr. Perfect, but eventually we all settle for Mr. Good Enough. And that's if we're lucky. My ex-husband wasn't even Mr. Nearly Good Enough."

Miranda grabbed her bag and headed for the door.

"Oh, well, home to Harold," she said with a sigh. She must have heard how that sounded because she stopped halfway across the gallery floor. "Harold isn't that bad really, but, like most artists, he's just a bundle of insecurities. That's why he needs me. I make him feel good enough about himself that he can create. I hope your guy isn't like that."

"I never get involved with artists. I've been down that road before," I said, waving as she went out the door.

For some reason, I found I was less excited about my date than when I had first walked into the gallery.

CHAPTER 10

I'm proud to say that I stayed in the gallery until the minute hand was directly on the seven. Even though I'd been tempted to leave a few minutes early, I had resisted; partly out of conscientiousness, and partly because I didn't want to arrive at the restaurant early.

Although it may sound depressingly traditional, I didn't want Mike to find me waiting in front of the restaurant for him. That would make me seem overeager, bordering on desperate. I might as well be wearing a sign saying, "Beware: Single Woman Approaching Thirty."

I took my time locking up the shop, knowing that if I walked slowly, I would get to the restaurant exactly at seven-twenty, right on time. Thus showing that I was a reliable woman of my word, not some high-maintenance, always-late Nellie, but at the same time implying that my time was valuable and a casual date had no special priority.

At least I hoped that was how Mike would interpret it. You never know with men.

After locking up, I slowly made my way over to Union Street. As I stood at the corner waiting to cross, my mind naturally went back to Mr. Peabody, who had stood at this exact same spot seconds before he was struck and killed. Again I asked myself, why had that couple been so anxious to get their hands on that Rafferty? So anxious that they were willing to commit murder. I liked the painting, but I wasn't sure I'd pay twenty thousand for it even if I had that kind of money. But this couple had been willing to go up another five, maybe even ten thousand. What did they know that I didn't? Was this Rafferty someone famous, and had Tompkins seriously undervalued the painting by mistake? Somehow Mr. Tompkins didn't strike me as a man who would fail to do his homework when evaluating a work of art. Underneath the somewhat vague exterior, a shrewd businessman must be lurking or the gallery wouldn't have been successful for so long. Miranda had told me that Tompkins had run the gallery for twenty years, and the profits had gone up each year from the one before for four of the five years she'd worked there. Last year had been the first exception, probably due to the off economy.

And why the mystery about "starfish"? Why would Peabody give me a secret password for handing over the painting? It was almost like he knew dangerous people were after it. It was like the Maltese Falcon of Safe Harbor.

I walked on several more blocks, unsuccessfully trying to fathom the problem, and quickly found myself in front of the Union Restaurant. Sitting on a bench a few doors down was Mike. I glanced surreptitiously at my watch and saw with relief that I was right on time.

Mike got to his feet and approached me, smiling. He was wearing a blue knit shirt, tan chinos and brown loafers. A very preppie look. Although his hair was still a bit unruly, it did look as if he'd run a comb through it.

"Hello, Laura. You're certainly looking lovely tonight."

"Thank you. You're looking very dapper yourself."

"It was nice to have a reason to get cleaned up," he said.

I wondered whether he normally got dirty in his line of work. Didn't he have much of a social life? These and a dozen other questions began swirling around in my head.

"I think we can go in. I made the reservation for seven-thirty.

You struck me as the kind of woman who would be right on time."

I smiled, thankful I hadn't decided to be fashionably late.

The hostess met us at her station right inside the front door and took us to our table. It might have been my imagination, but I thought she gave Mike a rather long look. Here I was on my first date with someone I hardly knew, and already I was feeling jealous. How pathetic is that?

We sat down at the table. The hostess handed us each a size-able menu, and said that our waitress would be with us shortly. I opened the menu and looked down the list of entrees. I hadn't eaten out formally since I'd been in Safe Harbor. Mostly, I'd gone to the local supermarket and cooked something simple for myself. I was a little shocked to see that the prices were comparable to Boston or New York. I looked up at Mike, wondering if it was fair to expect him to pay so much, especially when I didn't know what he did for a living. Maybe he was in a job that didn't pay much beyond the minimum wage. This one night out could cost him a week's wages. Then I told myself to be sensible. A man making minimum wage didn't plunk down two thousand dollars for a painting. All the same, I wasn't sure a date with me was worth a hundred-dollar dinner bill.

"I didn't realize how expensive this place is," I said. "I think I should pay my own way."

Mike shook his head. "I wouldn't hear of it. Dinner here won't cost much more than a knee and a hip."

"Don't you mean an arm and a leg?" I asked.

"I sell medical supplies, specifically orthopedic parts: artificial hips and knees."

"Oh. Now I see what you mean. Do you like doing that kind of work?"

"Sure. You're always telling doctors about what's new in the field. Sometimes I even get to be in the surgery to show the doctor how to implant the device."

"And you enjoy that?"

"I always wanted to be a doctor but couldn't handle all the schooling, and this is the next best thing. So don't be shy. Order whatever you want. It's all being paid for by the government and the medical establishment."

The waitress came along and told us her name was Emily. I ordered a glass of chardonnay and Mike asked for a Scotch and soda. I went through the menu carefully and chose the roast chicken, one of the cheaper items. Mike ordered the filet mignon. After the waitress left, we sat sipping our drinks for a moment, not saying anything.

"Do you live in Safe Harbor year round?" Mike finally asked.

"No, I normally live in western Massachusetts, near Springfield."

"Do you work in an art gallery there as well?"

"I work at a local newspaper."

"Ah, a journalist. What sort of stories do you cover?"

"When you're on a small newspaper you cover whatever needs covering. So I'm pretty much a generalist."

There was no way I was going to tell him that I was the advice columnist better known as Auntie Mabel.

"What about you? Where do you live?"

"New York City. Brooklyn, to be precise."

"Sounds exciting."

Mike shrugged. "The most exciting thing about Brooklyn is that you have a wonderful view of Manhattan. At least I do from my apartment. Or my loft. That's what it is really."

"So you have lots of wall space. Maybe I can interest you in some more art."

Mike smiled. "Only if you have another of those Rafferty paintings. I really liked the one you have in the gallery, but I guess that one is sold."

"In a manner of speaking," I said, and told him the story of Mr. Peabody.

Mike seemed to hang on my every word, and when I was through, he blinked several times and stared across the room.

"So this guy Peabody was murdered, then?" he asked softly.

"That's the way it looks right now. He was apparently killed by this mysterious couple."

"You lead an exciting life. Who would think being an art dealer could be so adventurous?"

"I certainly didn't."

"How did you come to get this job?" he asked.

I explained about how I had previously worked at a museum and how a contact there had known Tompkins.

"So why are you down here selling art instead of working on the newspaper back home?" he asked as the waitress appeared at the table with our salads.

"I just felt like I needed a vacation."

"No special someone back home who's pining away for you?"

"Not that special. How about you?"

"I work a lot of hours and spend plenty of time on the road, so it's hard for me to form lasting relationships."

That didn't make it sound as though we had much of a future together. I didn't know if I wanted to be just a vacation fling. Then I thought, maybe that was exactly what I needed, something fun and temporary with no responsibilities.

"How long are you going to be in Safe Harbor?" I asked.

"Well, I'm booked at the inn for this week. After that, I don't know. I have a couple more weeks of vacation, but whether I'll stay here or not depends on circumstances."

He stared at me as if I were one of those circumstances.

I began to babble a bit about the various things to do in Safe Harbor that might hold his interest, and was relieved to have a reason to shut up when the waitress brought our entrees. Mike took up the conversational gauntlet over dinner by telling various stories about medical devices, especially those times in the operating room where he had to assist the surgeon in placing the replacement part properly. The stories were scary but fascinating at the same time.

Before I knew it, we were sitting over coffee. I felt relaxed, as if we'd known each other for a long time.

"So what's going to happen with the Rafferty, now that the owner is dead?"

"The police said it becomes part of his estate, so I guess we have to hold onto it until his will is probated or whatever. Why? Are you interested in buying it?"

Mike shrugged. "I might be. But I'm not sure I want to be followed around by a couple of killers trying to get it from me."

"Well, it's on the wall in my condo right now. Miranda didn't want to keep it in the gallery because it disturbed her boyfriend."

"Are you sure it's wise keeping it there?" Mike said in a worried tone. "It might make you the target of an attack."

"There's no way they could know it's there. They think the Rafferty is still in the back room of the gallery."

"I don't know. These people seem pretty resourceful."

I nodded. "I wonder why they want it so much. I mean, it's a good painting but not famous or priceless."

"Yes. That is strange. Especially since they didn't exactly sound like a couple of art lovers."

"Right. They must be working for someone else," I said, suddenly realizing that must be true. But who could be the person behind them?

We finished our coffees and left the restaurant. The sidewalks that in a few weeks would be crowded with beachgoers were quite empty.

Mike took my arm.

"Would you like me to walk you home?"

"Not tonight," I said, gently but firmly disengaging myself.

"How about giving me your phone number so I can reach you?"

I recited my cell phone number. He punched it into his phone. Although he had written his on the receipt for the Rasmussen, I asked for it again and put it into my phone.

"And are you willing to give me your address?"

I paused for an instant and watched his face immediately grow anxious. I liked him, and we'd had a pleasant evening together. I still wasn't convinced I should give out that kind of information, but then I figured I had to show this guy I didn't think he was a serial killer. I gave him my address.

"Can I pick you up there the day after tomorrow for another date?" he asked.

I liked a guy who didn't keep you waiting by the phone wondering if he was ever going to call again.

"Sure. But don't bother bringing a car unless we're going outside of Safe Harbor. It isn't worth fighting for a parking space."

He gave me a little salute. "Whatever you say." Then he leaned forward and gave me a soft kiss on the lips. I could feel the blood rushing to my head and knew I was blushing. Mike just smiled and said good night; then he walked off up the street. I stood there staring at his back until I lost him in the shadows of the gathering dusk.

The air had gotten a little cooler after sunset, so I drew the shawl I was wearing more tightly around my shoulders and began to walk the eight blocks to my condo. Naturally, my thoughts were full of Mike, starting with the kiss then working my way back to our conversation over dinner. He seemed to be a good listener as well as a good storyteller. Not feeling comfortable admitting to being an advice columnist, I had told stories about my time working in a museum, and described some of my less personal adventures on the art scene. He had paid attention, laughed in the right places, and actually seemed able to appreciate in an intelligent way my view of art.

I was thinking warmly of his smile when I felt a twitch between my shoulders as if someone was looking at me. I spun around. The sidewalk behind me was empty as far as I could see, which was only to the end of the block. I took a few more steps then turned around again. Still nobody. I was walking up Beach Avenue so the ocean was directly on my left, while on my right were inns, currently empty. There was probably no one around for several blocks. I debated breaking into a run, but my shoes had heels that prevented running. I could take them off and sacrifice a pair of stockings. But running away from the invisible seemed foolish.

I threw my shoulders back, put some spring in my step and marched forward as though nothing was going to intimidate me. I never lost the feeling that I was being followed and that at any moment someone was going to rush up behind me and put an arm around my neck. I will admit that I did turn around a few times, only to find the sidewalk behind me to be empty.

If someone was following me, who could it be? Surely Mike wouldn't have decided to trail me just to make sure that I hadn't lied about my address. I thought of how Mr. Peabody had been followed before being killed, but I couldn't think of any reason why that couple should be coming after me. Plus, it would be a lot easier for them to run me down on the empty street than trail me on foot.

The more I thought about it, the more anxious I became, until my walk had turned into a trot. When I got to the condos I ran up the outside stairway to my unit and fumbled with the key, as it suddenly seemed to have forgotten how to fit into the lock. Only after I had gotten inside, shut the door firmly behind me, turned the security bolt and put on the chain did I begin to relax. I turned out the lights and peeked through the drapes covering my large front window. I'm three floors up, so my view of the street is limited. But I thought I saw a figure standing on the sidewalk looking directly up at me. I blinked, and he disappeared.

I closed the drapes and turned on the light. Then I went through the entire apartment to make sure I was the only one there and all the windows were locked. When I was finished and my hands had stopped shaking, I sat on the sofa and tried to reason with myself: I really hadn't seen anyone, I was overwrought from the events of the past few days, and I was overly excited from my first date in months. As I said these things over and over again, I actually came to believe them enough that after a cup of cocoa, I bravely went to bed. But I did leave a light on in the living room.

CHAPTER 11

The next morning was sunny and pleasant, and all my fears of the night before seemed silly and embarrassing. I had a good breakfast, which featured fond thoughts of Mike, and went off to work on the verge of breaking into song. I was still humming loudly to myself and considering an attempt at whistling when I saw the police cars at the back door of the gallery and my mouth went dry.

I rushed around to the front door and went inside. Miranda was talking to a man in a suit. I quickly glanced around the gallery, expecting to see it emptied of paintings, but nothing seemed to be missing. Finished with the man, who I figured must be a detective, Miranda walked over to me.

"I came in early this morning to open up and found that the back door had been forced open." She sounded calm but the tremor in her hands told me she was upset.

"How could anyone force that door? It has a really sturdy security bolt."

"From the pattern of the damage, the police think the security bolt wasn't engaged last night." Miranda gave me a long look. "Are you sure you set the bolt before you left?"

"Yes," I said automatically in a defensive tone. Then I stopped to think. Whenever I was on the evening shift and had to lock up, I followed the same procedure. I made sure the security lock on the rear door was set and let myself out through the front door, locking it behind me. Could I have done anything differently last night in my anticipation of a date with Mike? Might I have rushed out the front door without checking the security lock in back? I tried to recall, but all the evenings I'd locked up seemed to blur together. I couldn't specifically remember what I did last night.

"At least I'm pretty sure I did," I said to Miranda.

"It's not really important. Nothing very valuable was taken. The cash box is missing, but that didn't have much in it because I went to the bank yesterday afternoon."

"Were any of the paintings taken?"

"Not a single one."

The front door opened and Harold came rushing in.

"Are you all right?" he asked, charging up to Miranda.

"I'm fine, sweetheart. The police figure the whole thing took place in the night."

"Don't they patrol around here?" Harold asked, loudly enough to draw looks from a couple of the police officers. "Were any of my paintings taken?"

"I don't think so," Miranda replied.

Harold immediately ran over to the side of the room with the scenery paintings and began looking through them.

"Have you ever had a break-in before?" I asked.

"Not in the five years I've been here. The police think the burglar must have been a kid looking for quick cash to feed a drug habit."

"Still, it seems like an odd place to burgle. Most of the paintings here aren't worth much, and the few that are would require a specialized fence to get you any money for them."

Miranda shrugged. "Who knows why someone on drugs would do something? Maybe they just went from door to door looking for one they could open."

I nodded, feeling all the more guilty.

"All my paintings are here," Harold announced. His expression seemed disappointed more than happy, as if he had expected any self-respecting thief to want an original Harold Krass to fence on the black market.

"That's good, dear," Miranda said, not paying him much attention because right at that moment Mr. Tompkins came into the gallery.

"I called him only ten minutes ago," Miranda whispered to me. "He must be really upset to get here this fast."

Gone was Mr. Tompkins's vagueness of yesterday. This was a man on a mission. Giving the two of us a curt nod, he went into the back where the police were gathered. I heard him say, "I'm the owner here. Who can tell me what happened?"

I figured that once they told him their theory of the case, I'd be out of a job for having left the back door unsecured. To take my mind off the inevitable bad news, I walked over to the contemporary art side of the room and did a little inventory. I was pleased to see that the little Rasmussen Mike had put a deposit on was still there.

I was admiring it once again when I heard Tompkins say, "Laura, will you come over here for a minute?" I turned and saw him standing with Miranda by the front of the store. With a sinking heart I went over to join them.

"Did you leave the security bolt off last night?" he asked me as soon as I joined the group.

"I don't think so."

"Can you recall putting it on?" he asked testily.

"I think I do. But I lock it so automatically that I'm not sure."

He gave me an annoyed look. "And the two of you stand there telling the police that nothing in missing. When I was in here yesterday morning there was a large Rafferty sitting in the back room. Where is that, may I ask?"

"We decided it would be best if Laura stored it in her

condominium," Miranda said.

"And why did you think that was necessary?"

Miranda blushed and couldn't seem to find an answer. I knew she didn't want to admit the reason was that Harold went ballistic at the sight of the painting.

"We were afraid the couple who ran down Mr. Peabody might come back to try to steal it, so we thought it best to get it out of the shop."

Mr. Tompkins's eyes moved from one of us to the other. I could tell he was angry that we had moved the picture without his permission, but relieved that the Rafferty was safe.

"Well, I guess that turned out to be a wise precaution," he said softly. "Have you mentioned this theory about who the thieves might be to the police?"

We shook our heads. Mr. Tompkins herded us into the back of the gallery. Detective Geffert, a thin man in his forties wearing a suit, listened to our conjecture about what had happened. His eyes lit up when we told him about the possible connection to a recent homicide. I figured this break-in just went from a random theft to a case that might be a feather in his cap if he solved it. He said he would have a chat with Detectives Joiner and Belsen to see if they could shed any light on the theft.

"But if this couple wants that painting so much, it might be wise to move it to a more secure location than this woman's condo," Geffert said.

"Of course, you're absolutely right. I'll get in touch with my bank and arrange something," Mr. Tompkins said. "At the same time, I think I'll have a security system put in here at the gallery. I've been far too remiss about the matter."

"And, miss," the detective said to me, "remember a lock is only useful when it's used."

I nodded, not seeing any point in trying to defend myself.

We walked with Mr. Tompkins to the front of the gallery. I

was still wondering whether my saving the Rafferty was enough to outweigh my apparent lack of attention to security.

"Well, I guess this is one of those times when that old sports saying, 'no harm, no foul,' is applicable," Mr. Tompkins said with an odd expression that I took to be a smile on his face. "Be very security-conscious for the next few days until the new security system is installed, and I will look into a new home for the Rafferty." He turned to me. "Make sure your apartment is locked when you aren't there. That's a lot of money you have on your wall."

I nodded.

With a departing smile that was far more amiable than the expression he had entered with, Mr. Tompkins left the gallery.

"That was close," Miranda said when the door had closed behind him.

"For me at least," I agreed.

"For me, too. In moving that painting to your place, I went way above my pay grade. Normally Mr. Tompkins would be furious at me for doing something like that. But you gave him such a plausible explanation, it came out sounding like we'd done him a great favor."

"But, you know, now that I think about it, that explanation makes a lot of sense. If they wanted that Rafferty so badly, why wouldn't they break in here to get it?"

Miranda shrugged. "Maybe. But don't you think they've probably taken off by now to get away from the police? It's not that easy to stay lost in Safe Harbor."

I admitted she was probably right.

Miranda said she had a number of errands to run and asked me if I was too spooked to be by myself. I thanked her for the offer, but said I thought I'd be fine alone. After checking with the police, who seemed to be just about finished, Miranda left. The police departed about fifteen minutes later, leaving me all alone in the store.

I went over and sat down behind the desk. Oddly, I did feel rather alone after all the bustle and crowd of the early morning, but I decided the safest place right now was in the gallery because those who had killed Peabody knew the painting wasn't here.

What could it be about the Rafferty that made it worth burglary and murder? I turned on the computer on the desk in front of me and searched "Rafferty." After getting a few false Raffertys, I finally came to the one I wanted. There were thousands of entries under his name. Some sites showed pictures of his paintings; others posted articles about him. He even had a website that displayed some of his more important works. As I checked out his shows in various galleries, I was surprised to see that there had only been two, both in Manhattan.

From what I could tell from the various biographies posted, he was something of a recluse, an artist who didn't appear much in public and even kept gallery dealers at arm's length. In the only picture I could find of him, he was standing in front of a window with his face in deep shadows, obviously not a man who sought publicity. All of this was somewhat intriguing, but it didn't bring me any closer to knowing why this one picture of his was being so eagerly sought.

I turned off the machine and checked my watch. It was time for lunch. I put the "Closed" sign in the window and walked out on the mall. The warm sun felt soothing after the air conditioning and all the stresses of the morning. Down toward the center of the mall, I could see Angie sitting on a bench unwrapping her lunch. I smiled. It was nice to have some things, at least, remain predictable. Just as I had that thought a man came along, sat down next to her and gave her a kiss.

Chapter 12

I went into the shop and bought my sandwich. I debated over whether to take my sandwich and go somewhere else, leaving the lovebirds alone. But Angie would have expected me to show up, so she must have seen this as an opportunity for me to meet her boyfriend. As little as I might feel like meeting someone new at the moment, I couldn't very well run away and hide.

I walked toward them. They were both so engrossed in their conversation that at first they didn't notice me. When I was finally standing almost right in front of them, Angie looked up in surprise and performed the introductions. Stephen Anders held out a pudgy hand, and I gave it a firm shake. To give him credit, his own grip was solid, and his hand wasn't damp.

My first impression of Stephen was one of roundness. He wasn't obese, but he was plump. Everything from his chest to his arms was just a little more rounded than they ought to be. He had a round head on a sturdy neck, and his faced sported chubby pink cheeks. I had the impression that he might have a good sense of humor. I wondered at first if this was just my stereotyping overweight people as being jolly, but decided my judgment was based on his broad smile and friendly attitude.

"I'm glad to finally meet you. Angie has told me all about you."

I smiled, thinking to myself that after two weeks' acquaintance, Angie didn't know me *that* well.

"It's a pleasure to meet you. Angie says you teach elementary school."

"Fifth grade."

"That's a cute age."

"Yeah. The kids really want to be in school, and they still have respect for their teachers."

"I'm surprised you were able to get away in the middle of the week."

Stephen's ruddy cheeks got even redder. "To tell the truth, I took a sick day. I didn't want to wait until the weekend to see Angie."

As he reached out and took her hand, she beamed.

"You are devoted," I said. "It must take you several hours to make the trip out here from Philadelphia."

"Around two hours. I live to the east of Philly. The trip is pretty smooth right now before the high tourist season starts."

Angie leaned across Stephen. "We were hoping that we might be able to double-date tonight."

"Are you going to stay that long?" I asked Stephen.

"Sure. I don't mind driving at night. There's less traffic."

"I mean, we don't know how your date with Mike went last night, so we wouldn't want to pressure you," Angie said.

I took a bite of my chicken sandwich and chewed slowly. I was a little annoyed that she had told Stephen about my date. My romantic life somehow seemed too personal to discuss with a virtual stranger.

"The date went fine," I said after I swallowed.

"Good. We were thinking of going to the movies, to see that new romantic comedy, then go out for coffee and dessert. We could all meet at the movie in Westwood at six-thirty. Why don't you give Mike a call and see if he can make it?" Angie suggested.

I got to my feet and walked several feet away to make the call in private. If Mike thought this was a bad idea, I didn't want to discuss it in front of Angie and Stephen. The phone rang a couple of times. I was hoping it would go to voice mail. If Mike wasn't around, at least I could get out of this double date for the time being. Then Mike picked up and said hello.

"I was going to call you," Mike said. "I was thinking that we might do something tonight."

"I have a suggestion. Actually, I don't, but my friend Angie does. She wants us to double-date with her and her friend Stephen."

I had briefly mentioned Angie and her new friend to Mike last night. So they weren't completely unknown names to him. There was silence on the line for a second. Nervous, I rushed to fill it.

"I'll understand if you don't want to. I know it's kind of soon to be asking you to meet my friends. I wouldn't ask, if it didn't seem to mean a lot to Angie."

"I'll be happy to go."

"Really? You're not just saying that?"

"Well, I'll admit that I'd rather have you all to myself. But I think it might be fun."

"We're going to see a romantic comedy. Can you handle that?"

"That's my favorite genre after alien invaders. What time should I pick you up?"

"Six o'clock."

"Great. See you then."

I turned off my phone and headed back to where Angie and Stephen were huddled together like a couple of criminals planning a big score.

"It's all set," I announced. "Mike and I will be there."

"Wonderful," Angie said. The genuine enthusiasm on her face almost made me happy I'd agreed to the double-date thing.

And who knows, maybe it will work out fine, I told myself. Maybe Stephen and Mike will turn out to have lots to talk about.

I picked up my sandwich and resumed eating. I'd have been just as happy if the two lovebirds had ignored me, but Stephen must have felt an obligation to make conversation because he said to me, "Angie says you know a lot about art. Do you do any artwork yourself?"

I swallowed. "I dabbled in painting as an art major in college, but I realized pretty quickly that I didn't have much talent. I'm more interested in art history."

He nodded and focused his sincere blue eyes on me. "I had to learn something about art as part of my teacher training. It's really surprising how creative some fifth graders can be. Most of them draw exactly what's there, but others take a completely original approach. It's a shame that so many of them lose their love of school once they enter their teenage years."

I agreed that was a shame. "Angie told me you have a brother. What does he do?"

"My older brother went into the plumbing business with my dad."

"Did your father want you to be a plumber, too?"

His cheeks became a little redder. "What father doesn't want his sons to follow in his footsteps? Dad has always made a good living at plumbing, and I think he would have liked both of us to go into it with him. But he understood when I said that I felt that I had a calling as a teacher. But it's a good thing Dan, my brother, wanted to be a plumber. I don't think Dad could have handled both of us doing something else."

"I'm sure he wants someone to carry on the family business."

"Yeah, he thinks of it as his legacy."

Angie had been looking on with an admiring expression, as if to say, "See? I have a boyfriend who can carry on a conversation about something other than cars and sports."

"Stephen hopes to be a principal some day," she added.

"Not right away," Stephen said. "I've only been teaching for three years."

I judged his age to be about thirty, and decided there was a missing span of time in his resumé.

"What did you do when you first got out of college?" I asked.

"Actually, I didn't go to college right away out of high school. I went to work with my dad. He insisted that I give the job a try before making up my mind. I worked with him for two years, then went to college. It was probably a good thing. It made me a more mature student."

"How long do you have to teach before you can apply for principal?" I asked

"There's no fixed time, and it depends on when a position becomes available. But once I've got in eight years or so, I'd feel comfortable applying as principal of an elementary school."

I nodded. I had to admit I had a certain admiration for someone who could plan out his life in blocks of years like that. I had no idea where I wanted to be in eight months, let alone eight years. Maybe I should have worked in one of the trades right out of high school to learn maturity.

"Stephen is also talking about buying a house of his own," Angie added.

"Where do you live now?"

His cheeks got red again. "Well, I live with my parents right now, so I can save enough money to make a good down payment on a house."

"Sometime I'm going to go back with Stephen to where he lives, and we're going to look at homes together."

"It always helps to have a second opinion," Stephen said.

I kept my face as inexpressive as possible, even though I thought Angie was moving along far too quickly with this relationship. Two dates, and she's already picking out houses with the guy. Too much, too soon. I think Angie could read my mind because she gave me a petulant look. I finished eating my sandwich.

"Well, I'll see you both at six-thirty," I said, throwing my garbage in the trash barrel.

"I'm looking forward to meeting Mike," Angie said. By the look on her face I had a feeling Mike was in for a grilling.

"I am sure we'll have a great time," Stephen said, standing up and shaking my hand. "It was really wonderful to meet you."

I agreed it had been a pleasure, then I walked back to the gallery. I turned the sign from "Closed" to "Open," and went over to my chair and sat down. Here was Angie in a relationship with a nice guy who seemed to have long-range plans that involved her, a house with a picket fence, children, and a dog. And I was going out with a guy who didn't know how long he was going to be around, and whose long-range plans probably didn't extend beyond getting me into bed within the next twenty-four hours. Not for the first time, I wondered exactly where my life had gone wrong.

CHAPTER 13

When Miranda came in to relieve me at ten to four, I was still sitting in the same chair; however, I'd given up thinking about my future a couple of hours ago and was now reading a book on contemporary glass sculpture. It had marvelous pictures of several works by Dale Chihuly.

This was always the way it went for me. I'd think about my future, hit a roadblock, then find something more interesting to focus on. So I never made any progress in making plans. Is that a character flaw? Sometimes I think it's a sign that I'm not self-centered, which should be a good thing. Other times, as my mother would say, I think it just indicates that I'm unable to think ahead.

"No sign of our homicidal couple?" Miranda said it lightly, but the expression on her face showed genuine concern.

"The one place they can be sure the Rafferty isn't is right here. I don't think you have to worry about them paying you a visit."

"I guess I'm not really too concerned. But maybe *you* should be, with the painting hanging on your living room wall."

"No one knows it's there except for the police, you and Mr. Tompkins." And Mike, I thought, but he didn't seem to have anything to do with any of this. Although in the light of day and stone cold sober, I sort of regretted having told him. "Did you tell anyone else?"

Miranda blushed. "Well, I may have mentioned it to Harold."

I bit back an angry response. Telling Harold was like putting the news out in bold type on the second-rate painter grapevine. Who knew how many painters of terns, gulls, and plovers would know the location of the Rafferty by the time the sun had hit the horizon?

I took a deep breath. "It probably doesn't matter. I won't have it for long."

Miranda gave me a relieved smile, either because she believed my unconvincing blather or because she was happy I wasn't going to get angry at her indiscretion. I decided I would be very careful what I mentioned to Miranda in the future as I said goodbye and made my way to the door.

By the time I got home, it was almost four-thirty. Since I was getting picked up at six, I decided to have something to eat first. Going out for coffee after the movies always seems to turn into going somewhere with high-fat food and gorging yourself, unless you want to look like an anal-retentive party-pooper.

Being a relatively short five-six when I stand on my toes, I can't afford to pack on any extra pounds, so I decided that rather than having supper, I'd just have a bowl of cereal. So I poured something healthy into a bowl and covered it with the fresh New Jersey strawberries that were just coming in. I had taken my first spoonful when the doorbell rang.

I figured it was the woman next door. She owned the condo and was living there because she had separated from her husband, who remained ensconced in the family home in Cherry Hill. She moved out, as she told me repeatedly, so he could find out what it's like to deal with the kids on a day-by-day basis. Almost every day she would stop by to give me the newest episode in the saga. I really didn't want to talk to her right now, but I figured she'd probably heard me come in, and I didn't want to hurt her feelings.

I pulled the door open, a polite excuse already forming on

my lips, and saw the homicidal couple standing on my doorstep. He was still wearing a knit shirt that struggled to cover his girth and a pair of paisley shorts. She was wearing an attractive blouse and pair of slacks. Before my brain registered any more details, he jerked open the screen door and slammed his forearm into my chest. I bounced back hard against the wall but managed to stagger to my left into the living room. I grabbed the lamp off the end table, swung it over my head and brought it down hard in his direction. The lamp made contact, and I felt it shatter in my hands. There went my security deposit.

I looked up. The man's face was covered in blood. His forehead was opened like a ripe melon and his nose was bleeding profusely, as if broken. He staggered backward and covered his face with his hand. The woman glanced over and saw what had happened and her face twisted with fury. She reached in her bag and brought out a knife with a long, slender blade. I felt my abdominal muscles convulse at the sight of it.

The man made an indecipherable sound and pointed to the wall where the Rafferty hung. The woman nodded and began to approach me, carefully moving from side-to-side. I lurched backward, wondering whether I should turn and run for the bathroom. I could lock myself in and hope they would just leave with the Rafferty, rather than breaking down the door and slicing me up for revenge.

There was a flurry of movement by the front door and the man disappeared, as though pulled out through the doorway. The woman turned to her left, sensing that something was wrong. A man stepped into the room and gave her a casual blow that snapped her head back. Then his other hand grabbed her by the front of her blouse and dragged her outside. A few seconds later he returned to the room and carefully closed the door behind him.

"I let them run off. I hope you didn't want me to hold them

for the police. I don't do real well with the police."

"That's okay," I said, still trying to take in what had just happened. "Thanks for the help."

"They really didn't like you, Laura."

"They didn't care about me. They were after the picture," I said, gesturing with my thumb over my shoulder at the Rafferty on the wall. I stopped suddenly, wondering how he had known my name.

I took a long look at the man who stood just inside the door, staring down at his shoes like he was waiting to be recognized. He was a little over six feet tall and very thin in a hard, rangy sort of way. He wore a pair of worn jeans and a faded olive t-shirt. There was something familiar about him, but I couldn't quite put it together until he looked up into my eyes.

"Larry?"

"They call me Brew now from my middle name, Brewster."

"Laurence Brewster Stoddard," I said.

He shook himself like the name made him uncomfortable. But that was how I had known him back in college, where he had been the only art major on the football team, and the best running back they'd ever had. There had even been talk of the pros before he'd gone off and enlisted in the army right after graduation, surprising the whole school and particularly me.

"You waited for me," he said, giving me a shy smile that was a mere shadow of the confidant megawatt blasts he used to dole out to just about everyone back in school.

"What are you talking about?"

"I called your mother to find out where you were. She told me everything."

Mom always liked Larry . . . er . . . Brew, but what her opinion would be of this laconic stranger remained to be seen.

"What did she tell you?"

"That you haven't been married or engaged, and that you

don't even have a serious boyfriend right now. Isn't that true?"

"But that's because of bad luck, not because I was waiting for you."

He wore a puzzled expression. It came on slowly as if it took his emotions a while to catch up with what he was hearing.

"Why didn't you?"

"What?"

"Wait for me."

I looked at this thin sketch of my old friend Larry, one in whom all the wit, humor, and laughter had been taken out and replaced by fast reaction times and a penchant for violence. I was angry, and the emotion seeped into my voice.

"For one thing you never asked me to. You went off and enlisted without talking it over with me, then just came around and announced it one day when I was cleaning out my dorm room. You were so hopped up about going out and doing something for your country that you couldn't even be bothered to ask me how I felt. How your joining the army fit into my plans."

"I never asked you to wait?" he asked slowly.

I shrugged. "It must have slipped your mind."

"Would you have waited if I'd asked?"

"How long were you gone?"

"Six years. Two tours in Iraq and one in Afghanistan."

"To be honest, Brew, if you had asked me to wait six years for you, I'd have said no. Six years is a long time when you're twenty-two, and a lot of things can change. So no, I wouldn't have waited."

He nodded as if trying to make sense of my answer.

"And, Brew, I don't know how well you remember things these days, but we were never as serious as all that. We had great times in Boston and lots of fun goofing around. But I don't remember talking about marriage or having a future together."

"You don't?"

I shook my head.

He reached forward with one of his arms, blue veined and roped with muscle.

"I guess I thought it was kind of understood."

There was a sorrow in his voice that made me speak more gently.

"Over the years you might have talked yourself into thinking there was some kind of understanding between us, Larry. But there never was. I'm telling you the truth here. One day I woke up and you were gone. Sure, I cried for a while when I thought about you, but I never felt the great love of my life was over."

"I wrote to you."

"Three letters in the first three months. That was it. And I answered you. But all you wanted to talk about was the army and how great it was. There just wasn't much left for me to share with you."

He shrugged and looked unsure.

"Why did you come here?" I asked.

"I've been traveling around, seeing old buddies, mostly from the army but a few from the old football team. I thought that since I was in the area, I'd look you up."

"Where are you staying?"

"I haven't decided yet. I guess that sort of depends on you."

I glanced behind him.

"Where's your luggage?"

"My pack is right outside."

"Your pack?"

"Yeah, my backpack. I spend a lot of time hitchhiking and walking from place to place. If I'm in a hurry, I sometimes hop a bus." He turned and looked out my front window that faces the ocean. "I thought maybe I'd spend a little time enjoying the surf and sun."

I paused. To help me think, I got a broom and dustpan and swept up the shards of the dead lamp I'd hit the intruder with. Did I owe him anything for old times' sake? Maybe. Did I owe him for possibly saving my life ten minutes ago? Definitely.

"You can stay here for a couple of days. I've got a spare bedroom you can use." I made my voice sound stern, a matron laying down the rules. No hanky-panky here.

"I don't need a bed. I always sleep in a bag on the floor. I could crash right here in the living room."

"You'll use the bedroom," I said. "It's up to you whether you use the bed."

He gave me a nod. I wasn't sure whether it was a nod of thanks or a nod acknowledging I had decided to do the right thing. I went back to my kitchen table and began to eat my cereal, which by now was cold mush. As I was shoveling it in, Brew came in with an improbably large backpack.

"You have a lot of gear," I said.

"It's everything I own."

I thought I detected a note of pride in his voice, as if traveling light was a sign of superiority. I wondered if people who don't have much can be just as arrogant as those with a lot. I pointed him in the direction of the spare room.

When I was through eating, I checked the clock. I didn't have enough time to take the shower I had planned. If I rushed, I could be dressed and ready for Mike. I debated not going out at all, wondering if I should stay around to guard the Rafferty. But I decided Brew would provide plenty of protection.

I went into the master bath and put on my makeup, then squeezed into my best pair of jeans and put on my favorite red top. I glanced in the mirror and thought I looked pretty good, especially for someone who had been fighting for her life only an hour ago.

Right at six o'clock the doorbell rang. Mike was nothing if not punctual. I opened the front door and let him inside. When I turned around, Brew was standing in the middle of the room as if he had materialized from thin air. He gave Mike a slow onceover, as if sizing him up for a coffin. Mike, looking his usual rumpled preppy self, stared back with a bemused expression.

"Mike, this is Brew. He's my houseguest for a couple of days."

Mike nodded and put out his hand. Brew stared at it for a long while, as if wondering whether shaking hands with Mike was safe. Finally, they shook hands slowly, each of them staring into the other's eyes as if expecting a trick.

"Well, time to go," I said brightly.

Mike was the first to break eye contact. "Let's get on the road," he said.

"Have a good evening," I said to Brew. Then I want over to the table and dug through the sugar bowl until I found the spare key. I tossed it to him. "Lock up if you have to go out. But I'd appreciate it if you could hang around." I gave a meaningful glance in the direction of the Rafferty, and he seemed to get my point. I resisted telling him when I'd be back like he was my father or an older brother.

"Nice meeting you," Mike said.

Brew gave him a nod that showed little enthusiasm.

"Interesting guy," Mike said as we were going down the stairs from my condo to the parking lot.

"How could you tell?"

"Body language. He's very controlled, but with a lot of pent-up emotion."

"I suppose. He's spent a lot of time in wars recently. I guess that will do it to you."

"Are you old friends?"

"He used to be a boyfriend."

Mike nodded, but I could see a twinkle of mischief in his eye. "What?" I asked.

"Nothing. It's just that I've heard a lot of women keep in touch with old boyfriends. But I've never heard of one who had him living with her."

"It's not like that. He sleeps in the spare room. On the floor."

"On the floor," Mike gave a bark of laughter. "He really must want to be around you if he's willing to sleep on the floor."

"It was his idea. It's what he's used to from the army."

Mike smiled and shook his head.

"It's not funny," I said. "He's really sad."

Mike looked contrite. "I wasn't laughing at him. But you have to admit the whole situation is kind of odd."

"Well, it isn't going to last very long."

"Are you sure he's fully aware of that?"

"Yes," I said with greater confidence than I felt.

CHAPTER 14

Angie and Stephen were standing outside the movie theater when we arrived. I performed the introductions. It was interesting to compare the two men: Mike tall and relaxed; Stephen slightly shorter, rounder and more nervous. I thought Mike was clearly the more attractive of the two, but the way Angie cast adoring looks at Stephen, I didn't think she would notice. We went inside and got our tickets. Angie and Stephen bought the largest box of popcorn, while Mike and I went with the smallest.

The movie was entertaining but was so formulaic. It was like you were watching a movie you had already seen before. During the slow parts I looked across Mike at Stephen and Angie. He had his arm around her, and she was snuggled in close to him. They made me feel as though Mike and I were being awfully proper, but I knew we weren't at the snuggling stage of our relationship yet, if we ever got there.

After the show was over, we decided to drive up the road a couple of miles to a local place for something to eat. A hostess dressed far too elegantly for a highway diner took us to our seats and handed us huge menus. Mike and I ordered coffee and decided to share a piece of cherry pie. Angie and Stephen ordered colas and slices of the extremely thick chocolate crème pie we had passed by while making our way to the table.

"Those pies are never as good as they look," Stephen said, "but I can't resist them."

"The French say we do a lot of our eating with our eyes," I said.

"But Stephen makes a good point that things aren't always the way they appear," Mike said. He looked at Stephen. "Laura told me that you teach fifth grade. That must be a lot of responsibility."

"Yes. It's like being the father to twenty children. They become very dependent on you for things."

"With all that practice, you should make a great father in real life," Angie said.

Stephen blushed. "Well, it's not exactly the same thing. I didn't have to change their diapers or get up in the middle of the night to feed them."

"But you'd be willing to do that if you have your own, right?" Angie asked.

"Of course."

"You must have to know something about everything to teach fifth grade," Mike said.

Stephen nodded. "Pretty much."

Mike asked Stephen several more questions about his work, but got only monosyllabic answers. Whereas Stephen had been more than willing to talk about his teaching when it was only Angie and me present, he seemed much more reluctant to discuss his work with Mike. I wondered if he felt that his job wasn't masculine enough, and if this made him unwilling to discuss it in front of Mike. Although Mike was never anything less than polite, Stephen might well find him intimidating.

Angie must have decided Stephen wasn't being forthcoming enough, because she volunteered the information that Stephen hoped to one day be a principal. That made Stephen blush again, and he shot Angie a look that indicated he was sorry she had brought up the subject. He mumbled something about it being a long-range goal. Fortunately at that moment our pies came, and Stephen immediately directed his complete attention to that.

Mike and I began taking alternating pieces of our slice of cherry pie. Eating together seemed a very intimate thing to do, and I felt closer to Mike than I had all evening.

"Is the pie as good as it looks?" I asked Angie and Stephen.

"Definitely," Angie replied.

"Almost," Stephen said, putting another large piece into his mouth.

Angie stopped chewing and took a sip of cola.

"So I guess you met Laura in the gallery when you bought something there?" she asked.

Mike nodded. "Yes. And it's a much more abstract painting than I ever thought I'd want."

"It's not that abstract," I said. "The trees still look like trees."

"But they're pink and purple. You never see trees that color in the real world."

"Children are always coloring things in weird colors. They don't care whether it looks like the world or not," Stephen volunteered.

"That's okay for children," Mike said, "but I think adult paintings should represent the real world."

"Why try to paint like that when you can do it far more accurately with a photograph?" I asked.

"So you think photography has made painting obsolete?" Mike said with a smile.

"No. But I think photography makes representative art obsolete."

"So what's left for the artist to do?"

I paused, searching for the right words. "Maybe the job of art today is to present the world to us in new ways. So that we can find alternative ways of visualizing the world."

"Are you saying that if I look at my painting long enough,

eventually I'll start seeing pink and purple trees in the world around me?"

"No. But you might start noticing trees more and realizing that our minds are what construct the world around us."

"Whoa! This is getting way too deep for me," Angie said, digging into the crust of her pie. "Tell us something about what you do for a living, Mike."

Mike talked for a while about his work. I noticed that he didn't tell any of the same stories he'd regaled me with last night. I appreciated the fact that he didn't want to bore me. I was also amazed he had so much conversational material.

Finally, when everyone was through eating, we left the restaurant. We said our goodbyes in the parking lot and headed out in our different cars.

"What did you think of Stephen?" I asked as we headed back toward Safe Harbor.

"He certainly seems to be a dedicated teacher, and Angie acts like she's crazy about him."

"I know."

"You sound worried."

"It's just that she hasn't known him very long, and I don't want her to get hurt."

"Getting involved with other people is always a gamble, and there's always the risk of getting hurt. But what's the alternative? Never taking a chance on anyone?"

"No. But you have to be a little cautious and take your time to make certain that the person is who they seem to be."

In the light of the dashboard I saw Mike turn to give me a careful look.

"Yes. That is wise. But do we ever really know what someone else is like?"

"Not completely, perhaps, but you do get to know people more or less. You may not know with certainty what your best friend will do in a particular situation, but you can make a more educated guess than you would about a complete stranger."

Mike nodded. "That's true."

We traveled a couple of miles in companionable silence.

"Have you heard any more from the police on the Peabody case?" he asked.

"No, but I've had another run-in with the couple who killed him."

"What are you talking about?" Mike asked. The concern in his voice made me feel good.

I told him about the break-in at the gallery, and the attempted robbery at my condo later in the day.

"A good thing Brew was there," Mike said. "How did they know the painting was at your place?"

"Hard to tell. Miranda knew and she told Harold, who might have told others. I don't know who Mr. Tompkins told, or Geffert, the police detective." I didn't mention to Mike that he had known, because I didn't want him to think I suspected him.

"That was the Rafferty I saw on the wall of your living room?"

I nodded.

"You've got to get it out of there. Those people are persistent. Once they've licked their wounds, they'll probably come back, maybe with reinforcements. You can't wait until Tompkins has the gallery door reinforced. You have to get rid of it first thing tomorrow. Bring it back to the gallery if you have to. But get it out of your house."

"I'll take care of it," I said.

"Promise me. First thing tomorrow."

"First thing tomorrow. Cross my heart."

"And you have to report the attempted theft to the police. You should have done that right after it happened."

The thought of facing Belsen and Joiner again made me shiver.

"Do I have to?"

"You can't let a crime go unreported, especially when it's linked to a homicide."

"Okay," I said, knowing I sounded petulant.

Mike got a parking space on the street about a block from my place and walked me up to the front door of my condo. We stood there for a moment looking out toward the ocean, which was hidden in the darkness, except for occasional splashes of brightness when waves broke on the beach.

"I know you're not going to ask me in," Mike said.

"It would be a bit awkward with Brew being here."

"Ah, yes, the former boyfriend. But what if he wasn't here?"

"Not yet. It's too soon."

"You don't know me well enough. I could be something other than what I seem to be," he said, a hint of sadness in his voice.

"We've only been out on two dates. Give it time."

"Sure," he said with a resigned smile, "I can do that."

He reached forward and took me in his arms and gently but firmly kissed me on the lips. The boom of the ocean seemed to grow louder in the distance.

"Hmm. That was nice," I said.

"Do you have any idea how many?" he asked.

"How many what?"

"Dates it will take for you to get to know me."

"There's no set number. It will depend on how they go."

He frowned. "I hope I have enough time."

"I know you said you were here for a week, but you said you had a couple of more weeks of vacation that you could use. In three weeks we could get to know each other pretty well," I added hopefully.

"I'll have to see. In my line of work emergencies sometimes

come up, so I can't be sure how long I can stay."

"Artificial joint emergencies?" I asked.

"Sometimes a doctor will need me to be there during surgery, and I have to do it no matter what."

"I see. Well, we'll just have to hope for the best," I said, sounding cooler and calmer than I felt.

"Yes," he said after a slight pause. Then he gave me a small wave and went down the stairway.

CHAPTER 15

I don't know how long I had been asleep when a sound awakened me. At first I thought people out on the landing in front of the condo were arguing. But as I continued to listen, I realized the noise was coming from within the apartment. I rolled out of bed and opened the door to my room, wondering if Brew was talking on the phone at two o'clock in the morning. The sound was definitely coming from the bedroom; he was shouting at someone. I walked out into the hall. His cries were disjointed, as if he were in the midst of some disturbing event. I listened at his door for a moment then opened it a crack.

"Are you okay?" I asked softly. There was no response, just another flurry of cries for help mixed in with shouted requests for supporting fire. A long string of sentences filled with military jargon followed.

I backed out into the hall and turned on the light, then I went back inside Brew's room. I had enough light now to see that he was lying on the floor by the bed on an air mattress, rolling back and forth frantically and shouting out for help. I went over and knelt down next to him.

"Brew, Brew," I said softly, not wanting to frighten him. He paused for a moment, then went back to his dream. Finally, I reached out and grabbed his shoulders. I felt the muscles tense as he struggled to get away from me.

"Brew," I said more loudly, not letting go of his arm.

Suddenly he sat straight up and stared at me in bewilderment.

"What's going on?" he asked. "Where am I?"

"You're at my place, and everything is fine. There's nothing for you to be worried about."

"Laura?" he said, recognition flooding back into his eyes.

"That's right."

He caught me in a powerful hug. I let him hold on for a few moments, but then I became aware that I was wearing only a light nightgown and Brew was in only boxer shorts. I gently disengaged.

"Time to go back to sleep now, Brew," I said, pushing him back onto the mattress.

"Okay, Laura," he said, not offering any resistance.

I stood over him for a few minutes to make sure everything was going to be all right. Gradually his breath deepened and he seemed to drift off to sleep.

I returned to my bedroom and lay on the bed staring at the ceiling for a long time. I felt very sad about what had happened to Brew. I felt guilty that I had gone through my life mostly oblivious to the toll our wars were taking on soldiers. But I also knew that curing Brew was not a job I could undertake. His problems could only be solved, if at all, by professional care beyond anything I could provide.

How much responsibility did I have to see he received the care he needed? We had never been married or engaged. And despite Brew's apparent memory, we had never promised to stay true to each other in any other way. But did I owe him something as a former friend, as someone with whom I'd been very close to for a brief time in my life? I thought perhaps I did, but what that amounted to was something I puzzled over until I fell asleep.

The next morning when I went out into the hall, the door to

Brew's room was open. He was gone; however, his gear was neatly stacked in one corner of the room, so I knew he would return. His wallet lay open on the dresser. I glanced at it and saw a familiar picture in the plastic window. It was me, and I was wearing a bathing suit. I remembered the day it was taken when we went out to Cape Cod. I could feel the sun on my shoulders, smell the sunscreen, and hear the cry of the gulls. It had been one of those perfect days when the person and the place fit together to make an experience to remember.

I picked up the wallet, dusty and dog-eared. I felt the tears coming to my eyes at the idea that Brew had carried this picture of me through all kinds of hell. I cleared my throat. It was great if my picture had helped him get through the horrors of war, but that didn't mean that we were going to pick up where we left off. I wasn't going to be guilt-tripped into living someone else's dream.

As I put on the coffeemaker and pulled a box of cereal from the cabinet shelf, I gave some thought to my other major problem of the day: what to do with the Rafferty. I didn't see much point in bringing it back to the gallery until security was better, but it wasn't safe for me or fair to Brew to leave the thing hanging on my wall, crying out for another break-in attempt. What should I do with it? Suddenly, a little ditty sprang into my head, a song I'd heard on television for a local self-storage company. It took me a moment to go through the song to the refrain that gave the name of the company: UStore It. I grabbed the telephone book off the counter. Sure enough, there was a UStore It within a couple of miles of here. I took the Rafferty down from the wall and placed it near the front door.

I was back at the table eating my breakfast when the key turned in the lock and Brew came in. He wore shorts and a faded army-green t-shirt that was damp with sweat.

"Nothing like a run along the beach on a beautiful morning," he said. He gave me a smile that reminded me so much of the old Larry, my heart lurched.

"Yep, there's nothing like it," I said, returning his smile.

He pointed to the Rafferty by the door. "Making it easier for the thieves to take it the next time?"

"Harder, I hope. I plan to put it in a locked storage facility."

Brew stared for a moment like he wasn't following my train of thought. He took off his shirt and wiped the sweat off his lean torso, an action that derailed my own thinking.

"All that means is that next time they have to kidnap you," he said.

"What do you mean?"

"If they know you have the key to the storage box and maybe you have to sign in to get the box open, they'll take you along to get the painting. Once they've got what they want . . ." Brew made a cutting motion with his hand, which suggested that my prospects wouldn't be good.

"What can I do?"

He paused and thought for a moment.

"How about you give it to me to hide?"

"Won't that just put the danger on you?"

"True. But first of all I'm probably better able to handle it, and second, I'm a lot harder to find than you are."

I thought about his suggestion. It would only be for a few days until the gallery was reinforced, and I would feel a bit safer if the whole thing were in Brew's hands.

"Okay. Sounds like a plan."

Brew smiled. "Just let me use your car this morning to transport it."

"Do you have a license to drive?"

He frowned.

"I had to ask."

"As a matter of fact I do. I travel on foot and by bus because

I choose to, not because I can't drive."

"Fine. Sorry I said anything."

He grinned. "I know I sometimes make a bad impression."

"You seem a lot better today than yesterday."

"Yeah. Well, yesterday I was just a little tired, and I hadn't taken my meds."

I hesitated, not sure how much to ask. "So you are getting professional help."

He laughed. "I check in with the docs at the nearest veterans' hospital to get my prescriptions updated. That's all the help I need."

"But didn't you have some counseling when you came back?"

"For a month or so. But the meds were the only thing that really helped, so I figured why bother with the rest of it? As long as I have the meds, I'll work my way through my problems eventually."

"Like last night?" I asked.

Brew smiled and shook his head. "I wasn't sure whether that really happened or whether it was a dream. Having you there in my arms is something I've thought about for so long that I can't tell fantasy from reality."

"It was real enough, but so were your cries for help."

"Yeah. The demons can be the worst after you go to sleep and let down your guard. They come creeping up on you just like the enemy." He stopped and smiled. "But when the sun is out, everything is fine."

I nodded and tried to return his smile.

"So can I have the car, Mom? I'll only need it for a little while, and don't worry. You'll get that painting back whenever you want it."

I tossed him my car keys and looked at the clock.

"I have to go to work now. I'll be back in the afternoon, then I have to work the evening shift. Will you be here in the afternoon?"

"Hard to tell, now that I have to be elusive." He disappeared behind the kitchen wall then reappeared, laughing.

Whatever meds he was on, I could use some.

Chapter 16

The first person I saw when I entered the gallery was Harold. He was standing back, studying the largest painting I had ever seen in the store. It had to be four feet wide by three feet high, and it clearly dominated its side of the gallery, effectively hiding several of the smaller paintings.

"I call it *The Family Hour,*" Harold said, unable to take his eyes from the enormous picture.

Reluctantly, I walked over and stood next to him. The painting showed a sweeping panorama of beach and dune, in the middle of which were a male and female gull feeding a nest full of their young. In the distance the setting sun gave the scene a nostalgic look. With its anthropomorphizing title and golden glow, the picture was one of the worst examples of naturalist sentimentality I had ever seen. But I was sure some tourist would fall in love with it.

"I'm sure it will sell," I said. Harold beamed, as if that meant the painting was good. I had enough troubles without disabusing him of that notion.

"Is Miranda in back?" I asked.

"I'm right here," she said, walking out on the gallery floor. She glanced at Harold and her face took on an extra layer of concern.

"What's the matter?" I asked.

"I'm just not sure that Mr. Tompkins is going to let us show a painting quite that large. I told Harold to bring it in, and we'd see how it fit. But as you can see, it tends to overwhelm everything else."

"Don't worry about it. It will sell fast."

"Do you really think so?"

I nodded. "Somebody will have a large wall that just cries out for something to fill it."

"It *is* large." Miranda sighed, and I wondered if even she was getting a little tired of Harold the self-promoter.

"Actually we have an even larger problem to worry about." I told her about the attempted theft of the Rafferty from my condo.

"I'm afraid you'll have to tell those two wretched police officers," Miranda said when I was finished.

"I know. If you don't mind, I thought I'd go over to the police station this morning."

"Sure. I'll be here. You might as well get it out of the way."

"Another thing. Since the crooks apparently found out somehow that the painting is at my house, I've decided to hide it."

"Where?"

"I don't know. I asked a reliable friend to put it somewhere secure until I can bring it back to the gallery."

Miranda pursed her lips. "I'm not sure how Mr. Tompkins will feel about allowing a stranger to take charge of a twenty-thousand-dollar piece of art."

"I know the plan's not perfect, but the painting is a lot safer with my friend than it would be hanging in my living room. Besides, I don't want to be the target of any more burglaries. These people mean business." I described to her the woman with the knife.

"God, I don't blame you," she said. "They sound like they're crazy."

"They certainly want to get that painting at all costs."

"Well, I'll do what I can to get Mr. Tompkins to see it your way. And if he doesn't like your arrangement, he'll have to come up with one of his own. He has no right to expect you to get physically injured doing this job. Selling art isn't like being a police officer."

"And speaking of them, I guess I'll head over there."

I had just gone out the door and turned right to head up the street to the police station when I heard my name being called. I turned and saw Angie running up to speak with me.

"I just got a few minutes off from my boss, the slave driver, and I wanted to tell you that Stephen really likes Mike. He thinks you and Mike make a great couple."

I smiled. It was pretty presumptuous of Stephen to think he knew such a thing even before we did.

"Stephen seems like a very nice guy," I said.

"Yes, he is, isn't he?" Angie said. "He's coming out again in a couple of days, and we were wondering if you would like to get together again."

"Hmm. The thing is, Mike and I haven't really had much opportunity to be alone together."

"What about last night?" Angie asked with a wink.

"Something came up, and I wasn't exactly in the mood." I told her about the attempt to steal the Rafferty.

"And you didn't tell us anything about this last night?" she said, clearly annoyed. "That's not the kind of thing you should keep to yourself."

"In fact, I'm on my way to tell the police right now," I said.

Angie looked around at the crowds starting to walk through the mall.

"Yeah, it's hard to know who to trust nowadays."

"Well, I'd better be going. The police will probably think I waited too long already. I'll see you at lunch."

Angie gave me a wave and headed back up the street to the

store. I really didn't want to tell her about Brew. Somehow his story didn't make me sound like the responsible older sister. I could just see Angie's eyes going wide in surprise when I told her that a former boyfriend, who was now a veteran suffering from PTSD, was living with me. She'd never take any of my advice seriously again.

I walked up the street past the Victorian boarding houses where the day was just getting started. Busy homeowners were watering their plants, while the guests sat on the front porches digesting lavish breakfasts and deciding what to do during the day. Nothing happened very quickly in Safe Harbor. I hoped that Belsen and Joiner would see things that way.

A half hour later, I discovered that Belsen and Joiner were not quite so easygoing. When I first arrived in the police station and asked to see them, the desk sergeant made me wait in the lobby until he contacted them. They must have suggested I wait for them in the room usually reserved for serial killers, because the next thing I knew, I was sitting in a hard plastic chair in a windowless room that smelled of sweat and despair.

I stared at the dirty off-white walls and at the tabletop where someone had written "help" in jagged letters. I was beginning to understand how people could confess to crimes they hadn't committed after spending enough time in a room like this. I had plenty of opportunity to think about this and lots of other things, because Belsen and Joiner were clearly letting me stew for a while before putting in an appearance.

When they finally arrived, they were smiling expectantly, as if I were about to confess to being part of the gang that had killed Peabody. Joiner settled into the chair across from me, while Belsen leaned her hip against the table and stood over me. I figured she was the intimidator. It was working.

I took a deep breath and launched into my account of yesterday's attempted break-in. I told the story more or less truthfully, describing Brew vaguely as a friend who happened along at the right moment. When I was through, they sat there with smiles frozen on their faces, as if awaiting more valuable information.

Finally, Joiner took a breath. "So the same couple that killed Peabody tried to invade your condo yesterday, possibly to steal the Rafferty, and you, with the help of your friend, were able to drive them off. After which, you went about doing whatever you had planned to do without thinking to inform the police."

I felt my mouth go dry. "They were long gone by the time I could have called you."

"Did you see if they left in a vehicle? Better yet, did you get a license plate number?" asked Belsen.

"No."

"Of course not," she said with a note of triumph, as if I had proven her notion that I was absolutely worthless.

"Well, how did they find out that the picture was in my place?" I asked, angry and eager to challenge her and her partner.

"When they broke into the gallery and found the picture wasn't there, they must have figured out you took it home for safekeeping," said Belsen.

"That's quite a leap," I snapped. "I would have assumed that Mr. Tompkins, the gallery owner, would have it."

Joiner shrugged. "How many people knew you had the painting?"

"Five that I know about."

"And those five mention it to a couple of others, and before long the news is all around town."

I didn't respond, just sat and seethed.

"Where is the painting now?" Belsen asked. "Still hanging on your wall inviting a second attempted break-in?"

"I gave it to a friend to put in a secure place."

"Would this be the same friend who so valiantly beat off the crazed couple?"

I nodded.

"Does your friend have a name?" Joiner asked.

"Laurence Brewster Stoddard. His friends call him Brew."

"Of course they do," Belsen said with a snide smile.

"And where does Brew live?" Joiner asked, taking out his notebook.

"He's staying in my spare room right now. He's just passing through town."

"Wait a minute," Belsen said, hopping off the table and walking toward me. She leaned over me, so I had to look up to see her face. "Are you telling me that you gave a twenty-thousand-dollar painting to your transient boyfriend?"

"He isn't my boyfriend. He's just a friend."

"A pretty good friend, I'd say," Belsen said. "Do you know where he is right now?"

"Not exactly."

"How about approximately?"

"He's driving around Safe Harbor in my car, looking for a place to secure the painting."

"Or he's heading out of town with your car and the painting," she practically shouted at me.

"Brew wouldn't do that," I said. The words sounded hollow even to me. How well did I know Larry in his new form? Maybe he stole every day to support himself. The Larry I used to know wouldn't steal, but then, the Larry I used to know was a normal, middle-class kid.

"I wouldn't want to be you when your boss hears about your little security plan," said Belsen. "I have a feeling you won't be responsible for any of his paintings much longer."

The same thought had occurred to me.

Joiner pushed his chair back, making a grating sound on the floor.

"Ms. Magee, that painting is evidence in a homicide case, so I suggest you get it back from your friend as soon as possible." Joiner glanced over at Belsen, and I saw her give him a slight nod. "You should also know that the FBI has an interest in this case as well."

"Why are they involved?" I said, feeling the room suddenly getting even smaller.

"Their art fraud unit has a flag on this guy Rafferty's name. As soon as we put the name in our computer, we got a call. We faxed the Feebs our report, so don't be surprised if you get a visit."

"And they make us look nice," Belsen said.

I doubted that, but the FBI was certainly an added complication.

Joiner stood up, and Belsen went over to stand at his side.

"Thanks for coming in," Joiner said.

"Finally," Belsen added.

I stood up and looked at both of them.

"Is that all? What are you going to do to catch this couple that killed Mr. Peabody?"

"We have put out a description of them both," Joiner said. "Now we can add to it that the man most likely has a broken nose. He'll be more conspicuous with his nose bandaged. We'll also check with local hospitals and clinics to see if any heavy-set dude has had his nose set recently."

"He probably just had his girlfriend push it back into place and tape it," said Belsen.

I winced at the thought.

"These are not people to be fooling around with," Belsen said. "Next time you see them let us know right away instead of the next day."

I tried to hold my head high as I left, but I felt like I was slinking out of the room.

CHAPTER 17

When I got back to the gallery, I found Miranda, Harold, and Mr. Tompkins having a conversation in front of Harold's giant new painting.

"One week," Mr. Tompkins said, sounding as cranky as I had ever heard him. "You have one week to sell this *thing.*"

"Two weeks," Harold said, his beard jutting up at a stubborn angle. "I guarantee you it will sell in two weeks."

Tompkins turned slightly red, and I could see his jaw tighten.

"After one week, it goes behind the other paintings. After two weeks, if it hasn't sold, you take it back."

"Fine," Harold said, deflated and sullen. "But this is a great opportunity for you to become known as a gallery where you can buy monumental nature art."

"I have no desire to be so known," Tompkins shot back. Then he glanced over his shoulder and saw me. His jaw clenched even harder. "Ah, Ms. Magee, just the person I've been waiting for."

"Mr. Tompkins called and wanted to know the status of the Rafferty. I had to tell him," Miranda said apologetically.

"As well you should," Tompkins said, turning to me. "Your irresponsible handling of my property is a serious offense. Where is the painting right now?"

"I don't know." He turned even redder, indicating this wasn't the answer he wanted to hear.

Something in me snapped. I was tired of people blaming me

for losing track of the painting when I was the one who had risked her life to save it.

"I should think you would be a little more concerned about how I am after I saved your painting from those murderous thieves. After all, if it weren't for my friend and me, your painting, which we should remember is actually Mr. Peabody's painting, would be long gone. I think I deserve praise rather than blame."

I paused to take a breath. Mr. Tompkins stopped glaring at me and looked down at the floor.

"Of course, of course, you are right about that, Laura. It was very insensitive of me not to inquire after your condition. Were you injured in any way?"

"Fortunately, no. And you should also remember that you agreed I would hang the Rafferty in my home."

"Yes, of course."

"How did they find out that I had the painting?"

Mr. Tompkins and Miranda appeared stumped.

"Maybe they were watching the gallery and saw you take it home," Harold volunteered.

"That is a possibility," I said, surprised that Harold had come up with a sensible answer.

"Well, the real problem is, where is the painting right now?" Mr. Tompkins asked.

"My friend, the very same man who risked his life fighting off the thieves, has it in a safe location."

"And when will he return it to us?" Mr. Tompkins asked in a more reasonable tone.

"As soon as we have somewhere to keep it safe."

"Why don't you put it on your living room wall?" Harold said to Tompkins. "Then you can fight off the thieves."

"Harold!" Miranda said, horrified.

"No, no, he has a point," Tompkins said slowly. "It was selfish of me to let Laura take on that level of responsibility. I didn't realize the degree of threat here. If you will return the painting to me, Laura, I will put it in my bank vault where it will be secure. Do you think your friend would be willing to return the painting to me under those conditions?"

I didn't really know what Brew would do or not do. But I could only say yes.

"So when do you think I will have the painting back?" Mr. Tompkins asked, smiling.

"I'm not sure. My friend can be a bit hard to reach sometimes, but I promise you that I will tell him the next time I'm able to get in touch with him."

The smile had disappeared from his face.

"I would appreciate that," he said shortly. Giving Miranda a nod and ignoring Harold, he walked out of the gallery.

"Did you hear what he said?" Harold bellowed. "He said he didn't care if the gallery became known for monumental nature art. How can anyone be that dense?"

"Give it a rest, Harold," Miranda barked.

Harold looked startled, then his beard trembled, suggesting his feelings had been hurt.

"Do you really think you can get the Rafferty back from your friend?" Miranda asked.

"Of course. He's no thief. It's just that I don't know exactly where he is."

"Does he have a cell phone?"

"I don't know."

"So how are you going to contact him?"

"I know one place that he goes frequently," I said, not about to admit that it was my spare bedroom.

"I hope you find him soon. I don't think Mr. Tompkins is going to wait very long."

I nodded. "Neither do I."

Miranda walked to the back of the gallery, and I could hear her talking softly to Harold, probably apologizing for her harsh remark. I took out my cell phone. I'd turned it off in the police station and forgotten to turn it back on. I saw that I'd had a call from Mike. I was tempted to ignore it. I knew that Mike would want to know what I had done with the Rafferty. I really didn't want to go over my actions again, but since I'd spent the whole morning telling people the truth about what I had done with the painting, I figured that I should tell Mike as well.

I got him on the phone and, as expected, after the formalities, he asked how I had disposed of the Rafferty.

"I gave it to Brew to hide."

There was a very long moment of silence.

"Do you think that was wise?" Mike finally asked in a tightly controlled voice.

"I couldn't think of a better alternative at the time. Although now Mr. Tompkins has offered to put it in his bank vault, so once I get it back from Brew, that's what I'll do."

"Sounds like a plan. Of course, the painting doesn't actually belong to him."

"True. But somebody has to keep it safe until Mr. Peabody's next of kin is located."

"Yes, of course. Keeping the painting safe for the next owner has to be his first concern."

"I spoke to Angie earlier today, and she would like us to double-date again in a couple of days when Stephen comes down here."

A loud sigh came down the phone.

"You think that's not a good idea?" I asked.

"I've got nothing against Stephen and I like Angie, but I was hoping that we could have some time alone together."

"So was I. Could we get together tonight for dinner?"

There was a pause while I assumed he was mentally going

through his calendar. Of course, he could have been dreaming of a good excuse not to see me.

"Sure, tonight will be fine."

"We'd better make it seven-fifteen. I have to work this evening. Don't bother to pick me up at home. I'll walk to the restaurant directly from the gallery."

"What's the name of the restaurant?"

"The Crippled Crow. It's right off of Washington."

"Don't worry, I'll find it."

"And tonight is my turn to pay."

"That goes against all the rules of normal dating."

"Don't you know there are no rules anymore?"

"Okay. Well, we'll see."

"None of this 'we'll see.' I'm going to pay. And don't worry, the Crow is pretty reasonable."

"They don't specialize in carrion, do they?"

"They have a fine American menu."

After Mike hung up, I walked to the back of the gallery to see how Miranda wanted to handle lunch. When she was working in the afternoon, I would usually cover while she went to pick up something to eat. When I was working in the afternoon, she would cover while I had an early lunch with Angie. I found her in the back of the shop looking troubled.

"What's wrong?" I asked.

"I just don't understand what's gotten into Harold. All of a sudden he's furious with Mr. Tompkins for setting limitations on how long we can keep that large painting on display. He says that it shows Tompkins doesn't really have respect for him as an artist. Harold thinks Tompkins should be honored to show that painting in his gallery."

"Mr. Tompkins will look at Harold differently when the painting sells."

"Oh, do you think it will? It's awfully large, and Harold insists that we ask a thousand dollars for it."

"I'm sure it will take someone's fancy, and you can always negotiate the price."

Miranda's eyes lit up. "That's true. If Harold isn't here, he'll never know how much someone paid for it. Maybe I could sell it for seven-fifty and make up the difference out of my own money."

"That's a thought," I said. Not a thought I considered very progressive, but a thought.

Miranda still had a gleam in her eye. "I think this just might work. Harold is coming back to spend the afternoon in the gallery with me. At least I can be more upbeat now."

"If you're waiting for Harold, may I leave?"

"Of course," Miranda said, still smiling at her new plan to get rid of Harold's painting. I didn't have the heart to break it to her that selling one of these monstrosities would just encourage Harold to create more. I wondered at what point Miranda would consider it too expensive to protect Harold's fragile ego.

I didn't see Angie sitting at our usual bench, so after purchasing my sandwich, I walked down to the store where she worked to see if she was ready. When I went inside I saw her slowly pushing a dust mop up and down the aisles with the sullen look of someone sentenced to years of hard labor. Up by the cash register, eagle-eyed Mrs. McCrea was observing her every movement.

"Be sure you get under the counter bottoms, Angie. All sorts of things end up there."

Slowly but diligently, Angie ran the mop under the counters. When she saw me, her face brightened.

"Can I go to lunch now, Mrs. McCrea?" she asked.

"Finish the aisle you're working on, then you can go."

She turned to me. "How are you today, Laura?"

"Fine," I replied.

I hadn't felt comfortable talking with Mrs. McCrea ever since she had asked me privately a week ago whether I would consider leaving the gallery and working for her. I'm sure she was thinking of me as a replacement for Angie. She might have been right when she said that I was older and more mature than Angie, but I didn't think it said much for her opinion of me that she thought I'd do a friend out of her job.

"All set," Angie said, flinging down her mop. "I'll do the rest after lunch."

"Enjoy your lunch," Mrs. McCrea said to me more than Angie. I gave her a cool nod.

I made myself comfortable on our usual bench, while Angie bought her sandwich in the nearby store. By the time she came out, I had made my decision to tell her about Brew. The Safe Harbor residential community was so small that the least bit of gossip spread fast, and I couldn't trust Miranda not to mention something in passing that would give my relationship with Brew away. Angie was my friend, and hiding something that important from her would be a real test of our friendship.

"I have a man staying with me," I began.

Angie almost choked on her sandwich. "Mike's moved in with you already? Wow, you really do work fast."

"It's not Mike."

She stared at me. "You'd better start at the beginning and tell me all about it."

I told her about Brew, omitting the episode of his crying out in his sleep last night. When I was done, Angie looked at me with teary eyes.

"That's so romantic. He carried your picture around with him all the time he was at war. And I bet he's a real hunk."

I admitted that he wasn't bad in the hunk department.

"How can you not get back together with him after all he's been through?"

"I'm not going to have a relationship with a guy out of pity."

"But he's so committed to you."

"Not committed enough to talk over what he was planning to do before he did it."

"That's true," Angie admitted. "If I were going out with some guy and he went off and joined the military without discussing it with me first, I'd be kind of ticked. But I think I'd forgive him if he came back to me."

"Well, that's where we're different," I snapped.

Angie bit her lip and looked down at her sandwich.

"Sorry, I didn't intend that to sound so mean. But the thing is, Brew isn't the same guy I went with in college. Heck, he doesn't even have the same name. I hardly know him anymore."

"You could try going out with him and give him a chance. Maybe you'd come to like this new guy even more than you liked the old one."

"The war has left him really screwed up. I think it's more than I can handle."

"But don't you owe it to him to give it a try?"

I sighed and looked down the mall at happy people window-shopping.

"I don't know what I owe him anymore," I replied.

"It's pretty amazing," Angie said.

"What is?"

"Two days ago you were complaining because you had no one to go out with, and now you've got two handsome guys who want to be with you. You're pretty lucky."

"Yeah," I said. "I'm lucky."

CHAPTER 18

After having lunch with Angie, I didn't return to the gallery. I wasn't working this afternoon, so there was no point. Also, I'd had enough for the time being of the saga of Miranda and Harold, and being in the gallery just reminded me of the missing Rafferty.

I walked home at a nice slow pace, trying to enjoy the beautiful day. As I went along, I thought about how I was going to phrase my request to Brew that he return my painting. I figured he would probably be willing to return it to me once he knew it was going to be secured in Mr. Tompkins's bank vault, ending any danger to me. And to be honest, I'd be happy to see the last of that canvas, which had done nothing but disrupt my life.

When I got to my condo complex, I was pleased to see that my car was safe and sound in its assigned spot. I went up the stairs to my place.

"Hey, Brew," I called out softly, opening the door. I didn't want to startle him.

I was greeted by silence. I walked inside and stood still for a moment.

"Brew?"

No answer.

I walked across the living room and down the hall to the bedrooms. I went into the spare room. All of Brew's gear was gone. I checked all the surfaces in the room; no sign of a note. Then I looked all around the condo. Brew had disappeared without any explanation. I poured myself a cup of stale coffee, heated it in the microwave, then sat at the table and tried to come up with an explanation for Brew's disappearance.

The most depressing conclusion was that Brew had hit the road with a twenty-thousand-dollar painting, never to be seen again. Aside from the fact that I didn't think Larry, or Brew, for that matter, was a thief, I also didn't see where a painting would be easy for a guy like Brew to fence. I didn't know much about art theft, but it seemed to me that you would need contacts to unload a painting for cash. Contacts I didn't think Brew had. So why would he have decided to find somewhere else to stay?

The only idea I could think of was that Brew figured once I told people he had the painting, all possible danger would be directed at him. And in order to protect himself, he had decided to go into hiding. Since he hadn't left me any way to reach him, I simply had to have faith that at some point in time he planned to contact me secretly. I wasn't sure how much confidence I had in Brew, but since I had committed myself to him by giving him the painting, there was little point in having doubts now.

I changed into my running clothes, deciding that some exercise would help clear my head and ease my anxieties. The early afternoon sun was warm, but there was a pleasant breeze off the ocean and low humidity, so I was pretty comfortable as I made my way north at a slow pace along the boardwalk. When I reached the northern end, I turned around, ready to pick up the pace and make my way back. About a hundred yards away on the street parallel to the boardwalk, I saw a black SUV. The world is full of black SUVs, but I decided to run right toward it in the hope of getting a plate number just in case it was the one that had killed Mr. Peabody.

As soon as I started to run in his direction, the driver of the SUV made a sharp U-turn and sped away. That had to be more than a coincidence. My heart started beating faster at the

114

thought that I was being followed. What if Broken Nose and his girlfriend still thought I had the painting in my living room? And even if they had somehow found out that Brew had the picture, they might think that following me was the best way to find Brew. Either way, I was in their sights.

Keeping my eyes peeled for the SUV, I ran back down the boardwalk. I wouldn't put it past them to leave their vehicle and attempt to grab me right off the street. Every walker or jogger I passed got a careful onceover, and I remained ready to pick up speed in a flash if necessary. I might not be able to beat Broken Nose in a fair fight, but I was pretty sure I could outrun him.

When I got back to my condo, I put on the safety bolt and the chain, then sat in my kitchen wondering what to do. As I slowly calmed down and my heart rate returned to normal, I began to feel very sleepy. My rest last night had been disturbed by Brew's shouting, and the day so far hadn't been exactly relaxing, so I went in the bedroom and lay on the bed, half convinced that I was far too nervous to sleep. Within a few minutes I was gone.

I woke up feeling rested. I looked at the clock and saw that I had slept for an hour. I stretched languorously, feeling at peace with the world, until I remembered my situation. My gut tensed and I jumped from the bed. I went to the front window and peeked out around the curtain to see if anyone was out there watching me. I could see the parking lot and a good part of the street in front and didn't notice anything suspicious.

I took a shower, keeping the bathroom door open to better hear what might be going on in the condo. I got dressed, again a little fancier than usual because of my date with Mike, and had a bowl of cereal to tide me over until dinner. I decided to take my car to work because that would give my stalkers less of an opportunity to grab me off the street. I studied the parking lot for several minutes from my living room window to make sure no one was waiting out there. When reasonably convinced that everything was normal, I walked quickly down the outside stairs to my car. I glanced around as I opened the door, but didn't see anything suspicious. Once in the car I locked the doors and took a deep breath.

I drove to work, looking repeatedly in my rearview mirror for signs of the SUV. I parked behind the gallery. Two men had the gallery's back door off its hinges and were getting ready to replace it with another that was leaning against the wall. I walked around to the front and went inside. Miranda came out from the back.

"I see the men are here working on security," I said.

"Yes. They're putting a new door on the back today. Tomorrow we get an upgrade to the locks on the front door and a state-of-the-art security system."

"That sounds good."

"As of tomorrow, we'll have a system that connects directly to the police department. All because of one painting."

"And one murder."

"Of course. I shouldn't forget poor Mr. Peabody."

"Was there much business this afternoon?" I asked.

"No. But I did have a couple express some serious interest in Harold's giant canvas."

"Great. What happened?"

"They were only willing to go as high as seven hundred."

"Weren't you going to make up the difference to reach a thousand?"

"I've decided that the painting has to bring in eight hundred. I'm willing to throw in two, but no more and hopefully less." Miranda smiled. "Who said you can't put a price on love? Here I am saying that my boyfriend's success is only worth two hundred dollars to me."

"You're still being generous."

"I only wish Harold would talk things over with me first. You know, I had no idea he was going to bring that picture in today," Miranda said, waving her hand in the direction of the huge canvas. "If I'd known, I would have told him we should discuss it with Mr. Tompkins before moving it into the gallery. But you know Harold. Like a lot of artists, he isn't very good when it comes to dealing with people. And the way he was so rude to Mr. Tompkins today just shocked me. If he keeps that up, Tompkins may decide not to carry his work anymore."

"There are other galleries."

"But almost all of them have their full quota of artists by this time of year. Harold would find it very hard to fit in someplace else."

I looked at Harold's picture. "I guess he's just following his muse, and it told him to work bigger."

"He should follow his common sense. This gallery isn't equipped to carry monumental-sized works."

I wondered if Miranda and Harold were about to come to a parting of the ways. I had never heard Miranda speak so critically of him before. It sounded as if they were just one more large painting away from breaking up. I found that, in an odd sort of way, I wanted them to stay together. I thought down-to-earth, balanced Miranda was a good counterpoint to off-the-wall, creative Harold. I also suspected they were happier together than they would be apart.

"Maybe if you just sat down and explained things to Harold, he would understand why he should run things by you first and be more diplomatic with Mr. Tompkins."

"Explaining anything to Harold takes a huge effort, and when it comes to art, it's even worse because he can be amazingly stubborn."

"You've got no choice. You have to give it a try. You can't stand by and let Harold destroy his career."

Miranda looked once again at the large painting. "You're right. Harold's too talented. I can't allow him to waste his gift."

I wouldn't go that far, I thought, biting my tongue.

"Tonight we are going to sit down and have a heart-to-heart. Thanks for the advice, Laura."

"No problem." I figured by tomorrow, they'd either be a stronger couple or no couple at all.

After Miranda left, I walked in the back and introduced myself to the men who were working on the back door. They were too busy to pay much attention to me, but when five o'clock came and they told me they were leaving for the day, it was with genuine regret that I watched them go. At least with them here I had felt relatively secure. Once they were out the door, I kept expecting my assailant couple to show up ready to torture me into telling them what I didn't know: the location of the Rafferty.

The couple that did come through the door didn't frighten me, but they certainly appeared strange. A man and a woman, both in their late thirties, they wore dark business suits, not exactly everyday wear at the beach. His hair was short enough to be almost military; hers was short but not so short as to be mistaken for punk.

"Are you Laura Magee?" the woman asked in a sharp, clear voice more suitable for the stage.

I admitted I was.

"We're from the Federal Bureau of Investigation," the man said. They both held out wallets that contained something looking official. "I'm Agent Ganz and this is Agent Spilker."

"How can I help you?" I said in something close to a stammer.

"We have reason to believe that you were recently involved in the sale of a painting by Rafferty," Agent Spilker said. Somehow she made it sound like I'd been involved in the sale of something illegal.

"We had one for sale in the gallery, and I sold it. That's what I do," I replied.

"Of course," Agent Ganz said soothingly. "We didn't mean to imply that you had done anything wrong."

"We also have come to understand that the man you sold the painting to died under suspicious circumstances," the female agent said.

"There was nothing suspicious about it," I said. "He was run over by two people in an SUV who later attempted to steal the painting from me."

"Yes. We've read the police report and had a chat with Detectives Belsen and Joiner," the woman said. I would like to have seen that conversation. She and Belsen struck me as two of a kind.

"We were wondering if the dead man, Arthur Peabody, said anything to you about representing someone else."

I thought about starfish, but didn't say anything. I didn't think that would help them, and I still thought of the code word as something told to me in confidence.

"No. As far as I knew, he purchased the painting for himself. Why do you ask?"

I thought Spilker was about to tell me to mind my own business, but at that moment Agent Ganz, who had been glancing around the gallery, suddenly focused in on our conversation.

"Let me give you a little bit of background on this, so you can see what we're up against," he said, flashing a we're-all-in-this-together smile.

I nodded.

"Dennis Rafferty approached us about a month ago. He claimed that there had been a couple of attempts on his life. Nothing overt. They both could have been construed as accidents, but he had concluded otherwise."

"Why would anyone want to kill an artist?"

"A very good question, and this is where Rafferty's story gets interesting. He claimed that a number of his paintings had sold over the last few years to people who were untraceable. They either paid cash or, if they used a credit card, it was in the name of a dummy corporation that could only be traced back to an offshore account."

"How did Rafferty find all of this out?" I asked.

"He hired a private investigator."

"And then he came to see you. Why the FBI?"

"He approached us through our Art Frauds Division. It was his contention that some individual or entity was buying up Raffertys. It was their plan to kill him, and then wait a few years until his paintings appreciated in value before selling them on the open market. As you doubtless know, nothing causes a work of art to appreciate like the death of the artist, because everyone knows there won't be any more work from that source. Think of Jackson Pollock."

I shook my head. "The whole thing sounds pretty farfetched to me. And Jackson Pollock was a recognized genius before his death. I'd never even heard of Rafferty."

"Then you haven't heard enough," Spilker snapped. "He's a real up-and-comer. Right on the edge of breaking into the big leagues."

"We think," Ganz said softly, trying to diffuse his associate's hostile edge, "that Rafferty is the ideal candidate for something like this. He's not so famous that the art world would be stunned if one person or gallery had the lion's share of his work. They would simply be considered lucky to have spotted talent at its inception, and no one would accuse them of any kind of inappropriate activity."

"So what did your people do to investigate Rafferty's allegations?"

"Unfortunately, not very much," Spilker said. "Let's say that the agent who first took down the report shared your point of view that it was farfetched. He put out a flag on Raffertys, so if any were reported as part of a crime, the news would jump out on our computer. But other than that, he did nothing."

"I'll bet Rafferty is telling you 'I told you so' right now."

Ganz shook his head. "Rafferty isn't telling us anything because he's disappeared."

"Do you think he's dead?" I suddenly felt very sad. Although I didn't know Rafferty, I knew one of his pieces. He was definitely talented, and the death of a talented person is always a great loss.

"There's no evidence that he's dead," Ganz said in an aggrieved tone, as if it was Rafferty's fault for not being helpful and surfacing as a corpse.

"What about Arthur Peabody? Where does he figure in all of this? Surely he wasn't one of these people trying to buy up Raffertys." I hoped he wasn't. I didn't like the thought of that kind man being part of an art scam.

"We don't think he was part of it," Ganz said. "First of all, Peabody was his real name, and he had an easily traceable identity. He was a painter himself, and he lived in Queens, New York. It's very plausible he came down to Safe Harbor on vacation and decided to buy a Rafferty."

"Except for one thing," Spilker said. "He was apparently living on his Social Security and what he made doing some teaching and the occasional sale of a painting. We've checked his bank records, and he received a sudden and mysterious infusion of cash, over thirty thousand, just last week. Without that, he never would have been able to pay for that Rafferty."

Ganz nodded. "That's why we asked you if he had given any

indication that he was representing someone else."

I frowned. "But if he wasn't one of the bad guys, whom would he be representing?"

"We don't know," Ganz admitted. "But we're hoping that if we can keep an eye on this painting, we may be able to find out who has been buying all those Raffertys and who plans to kill, or already has killed, the painter."

"But if he were already dead, wouldn't they have wanted his body to be found, so he could definitely be declared dead?"

Ganz smiled. "Just what we thought. That's one reason we're not convinced Rafferty is deceased."

Spilker's eyes were surveying the gallery.

"So where is this Rafferty?" she asked.

I sighed and told them most of the story about the painting, its attempted theft, and how it ended up with Brew.

"Are you sure you didn't make a deal with this couple to sell them the painting? And then make up the story about a wandering hobo veteran, just to cover what happened to the picture?" Spilker asked, moving close to me and virtually shouting in my face.

"That's nonsense," I said, trying to keep my lip from quivering. My entire face felt numb, and I was sure I looked like the poster girl of an art thief.

Ganz stepped in and touched my arm lightly. "No one thinks you're a thief. But you have to admit that it might not have been wise to let this fellow Brew take charge of the painting."

"It was either that or have to face the homicidal duo one more time. And from what you're telling me now, they could be part of some international plot."

"They were probably the ones who were supposed to buy the Rafferty for their crime boss, but they got there a few minutes too late," Ganz said. "Then they decided to kill Peabody, hoping to find the painting in his room. Now they've traced it to you. The fact that you don't actually have it isn't going to stop them from forcing you to tell them where it is."

"I don't know where it is."

"Even we don't believe that," Spilker said, her short hair bouncing as she shook her head. "They certainly aren't going to swallow that story."

I was about to say it was the truth, but I decided I would just sound pathetic. Instead, I shrugged helplessly.

"Is there any way you can get in touch with Brew?" Ganz asked.

"No."

"But you think he will be contacting you soon."

"I think so," I said hopefully.

Spilker gave a disgusted grunt.

"Good. Once we have that painting, we can set up some kind of a trap that will let us capture at least a couple of the low-level people."

"Or maybe you could let them get away with the painting and follow them back to the big guy," I suggested.

"But in order to do either of those things, we have to get that painting back," Spilker said, staring hard at me.

"I'm sure Brew will get in touch with me soon," I said.

Ganz took a card out of the inside pocket of his jacket and handed it to me.

"Give us a call as soon as you hear anything."

I nodded. Ganz gave me a friendly smile, while Spilker turned away as though I had ceased to exist for her. Yeah, I figured, she and Belsen must have had a great conversation. Sometimes being sisters under the skin doesn't lead to harmony.

CHAPTER 19

I spent the rest of my time at work pacing back and forth from the front to the back of the gallery. I'd look out the front window, my eyes peeled for a fat man with a bandaged nose or a woman in a sundress carrying a knife in her bag. Then I'd walk to the back of the studio and wonder what good a newly reinforced door was going to do for me when the gallery was open to the public. Back and forth I went, wearing a path in the tile.

I nearly jumped out of my skin when a couple with two young children actually opened the door and walked in. After I got my breath back, I greeted them, told them to feel free to look around, and said I would answer any questions they had. The parents went off to check out the goods, but the two children, one boy and one girl, stood amazed in front of Harold's enormous painting.

"Birds, birds," they alternately repeated. The little girl, who appeared to be about three, reached out her hand as if to touch the birds, but stopped just short of the canvas. I thought it was only a matter of time before the boy, who was a couple of years older, actually did touch the thing.

I walked over to stand next to them. This wasn't a museum where bells and whistles went off if a painting was touched, and a child's hand wouldn't diminish the artistic significance of Harold's work. But I didn't want anyone poking a hole through a painting on my watch.

"They do look real, don't they?" I said to the children in that overly bright voice adults use with the young. The little girl stuck her index finger in her mouth and nodded solemnly. The little boy ignored me, but I could see his hand creeping steadily closer to one of the birds.

I was about to say something stupid to the boy along the lines of not frightening the birds when a man's voice said, "Maxwell, don't touch the pictures."

The boy's hand fell as his father walked up behind him with the woman at his side.

"The children seem fascinated with that picture," she said.

"Probably because everything in it is bigger than life size. It must look huge to them," the father said.

I wanted to say that the birds looked pretty huge to me, too.

"We could really use something large for over the sofa in the family room," the woman suggested.

"But a thousand dollars?" the man whispered.

"How much did you spend for those new golf clubs?" she whispered right back.

The man frowned irritably. "They're made of titanium. They'll last forever."

"Or until the next new thing comes along. We'd have this painting for at least as long."

The little girl was staring hard at one of the birds in the nest and began to make a contented cooing sound.

"Emma seems very taken with it," the woman added.

At that moment, the boy reached up and actually touched one of the birds. The painting gave a shallow ripple along its length.

"Stop that, Maxwell," the man said. He turned to me. "Sorry about that."

"Not a problem," I said. "Your children seem hypnotized by the painting."

"I've never seen them interact that way with any of our pictures at home," the woman said.

"It's probably the size," I said.

"The price is pretty big, too," the man added.

I nodded. "More paint, more canvas, and more of the artist's time."

"Does it come with the frame?" the wife asked.

I assured her that it did. I could see by her expression that the wife was already sold, and the husband knew it. But he couldn't go along with her without getting some concession.

"Next week we're going to start a twenty percent off sale on selected paintings. But if you buy this painting today, I'll give you the twenty percent."

"Eight hundred," the man said thoughtfully.

I nodded. He paused to mull it over, so I changed the subject and said to his wife, "Is Maxwell in school?"

"Yes, first grade."

"When does he get out for the summer?"

"We live in Philadelphia, so he got out at the end of last week."

"I think we should go for it," the man suddenly said. He looked at his wife, who nodded her head happily, probably wondering what had taken him so long. "Can we carry it away with us now?" he asked.

I assured them they could, and twenty minutes later—it took that long to wrap the monstrosity—I held the door as, between them, they carried the picture out of the gallery and down the street. I hoped their car wasn't far away. After they left, I looked up at the clock and happily saw it was time to leave. I checked the back door, which now seemed very secure with its new lock, then went out the front, locking the door behind me. I walked around to the back of the shop to retrieve my car. After hitting a bit of congestion right at the main intersection at the end of the mall, I sailed along for the next six blocks and got a parking space on the street a block or so from the Crippled Crow.

I don't know exactly how the Crippled Crow got its name. The sign hanging from the front of the building showed a crow with a small crutch under one wing, but I was told the sign was put up by the most recent owner. Miranda said she heard that back in the early nineteenth century, when the place was a tavern and inn, the owner kept an injured crow in a cage and that's how the name got started. I didn't really care. The food was good and quite reasonable for a resort area.

When I was about half a block away, I saw Mike standing in front of the restaurant. He was pacing back and forth and looking all around him as if on the alert for something. When he saw me approach, he smiled.

"I was afraid something had happened to you," he said.

I glanced at my watch. "I'm only five minutes late. I had to park down the street."

"After you told me about those people trying to steal that painting, I was afraid you'd had another run-in with them."

"Fortunately not. But I did have a visit from the FBI."

Mike appeared stunned. "Really? How did they get to be involved in this?"

I took his arm and guided him toward the door. "Why don't we go inside and get a table, and then I'll tell you all about it?"

Twenty minutes later, between drinks and eating our salad, I had brought Mike up to speed. He had asked detailed questions and shaken his head several times in amazement.

"I can see why the FBI didn't believe this guy Rafferty when he came in with that story. It sounds pretty wild," Mike said as our entrees arrived.

"Not really. After an artist dies, if his work was selling pretty well during his lifetime, it will skyrocket in value. If somebody had a horde of Raffertys, they could be worth three or four times as much after his death than they do now. That's a pretty good return on investment."

"And nobody would be suspicious?"

"Not if his death appeared accidental or if there was no link between the owner of the works and the death of the artist."

"Do you think you'll be able to get the painting back from Brew, so the FBI can set up a trap?"

"I'm sure Brew will contact me sometime. I just don't know when."

"And this fellow Peabody wasn't part of the scam?" he asked, taking another roll from the wicker basket.

"He doesn't seem to have been buying for the folks planning to kill Rafferty. In fact, it looks like they killed him. But he didn't have enough money to buy that Rafferty himself, so he must have been working for somebody."

"And Rafferty himself has disappeared, is that right?"

"Either he's disappeared or been murdered. It would be a shame if that has happened."

"Why is that?" He paused for a moment when I looked at him strangely. "I mean, I realize the death of an innocent person is always unfortunate, but is there any other reason for sadness?"

"I think he's a very good artist."

He nodded. "What concerns me more right now is your safety. Those killers still think you have the Rafferty, and it's only a matter of time before they come after you to get it."

"I can't help them."

"But as everyone keeps telling you, that won't matter. They'll use you in some way to try to get the painting back from Brew, and the experience probably won't be pleasant. You haven't forgotten that woman with the knife."

An involuntary contraction of my abdominal muscles told me I hadn't.

"What can I do about it?"

"Don't go home."

I laughed. "Is this where you tell me that I'd be safer staying at your place instead?"

Mike blushed and looked a little hurt.

"As a matter of fact, you would be safer."

I reached across the table and took his hand.

"I'm sorry. I know you really are concerned about me. And the idea of staying with you is actually very appealing. The problem is that then Brew would have no way of finding me. I have to stay on the radar until I get the painting back."

"I know you're right. And I'm honestly not using this as a way of seducing you. I just wish there were some way to get you out of the line of fire."

"Once I get the painting back, I'll turn it over to the FBI and let them take it from there."

We finished eating and both of us passed on coffee and dessert. I didn't need caffeine keeping me awake when I had a couple of murderers on my mind; nor did I need the extra calories of a scrumptious dessert. In fact, I was carrying half of my dinner home with me in a plastic container. That told me how serious things had become when they started to affect my appetite. I had to almost arm-wrestle Mike for the check. He only agreed to let me pay for our food when I promised to have dinner with him again soon, and let him pay.

We walked out the front door of the restaurant and stood by the curb.

"I could drive you back to your condo. If I were there with you, you'd be safer and Brew would be able to find you."

For a moment that idea sounded attractive, but I still didn't know how deeply involved I wanted to be with Mike. Even though we'd been out on several dates, I still didn't feel I knew him all that well. I also wasn't sure how much help he would be against a couple of armed intruders. I didn't want to have to worry about him as well as myself.

"I don't want to leave my car parked on the street overnight."

"Well, at least let me walk you to your car."

I agreed. As we started to cross the street, a black SUV I hadn't seen before pulled out from the curb and began speeding down the road toward us. I back-pedaled furiously, losing all sense of where Mike was. The vehicle passed us closely enough that I felt the breeze. It raced down to the next corner where it took the turn with a screech of brakes and disappeared. Having a chance to look around me, I saw Mike lying on the ground a few feet away, and my heart nearly stopped.

"Are you okay?" I asked, rushing to him and helping him to stand. He wobbled, threatening to fall down, so I helped him sit on the curb.

"I jumped backward, but then I fell and hit the back of my head on the curb," he said, touching his head and wincing.

A man rushed up to us. "We saw what happened and called the police."

I thanked him and asked Mike if he was experiencing any dizziness or light-headedness.

"No, but I bet I'm going to have a terrific headache," he said plaintively.

And so am I, I thought, once Belsen and Joiner get wind of this.

CHAPTER 20

"If they had wanted to kill you, you'd be dead," Detective Belsen said with a sad look, as if she were sorry I'd survived.

"How do you figure?" I asked, taking a sip from my glass of water.

We were sitting in a small office off the lobby of the restaurant. The uniformed officers who answered the call had somehow known to notify my two favorite people on the force. Mike had been examined by the EMTs and declared probably fit, but he was taken to the hospital overnight for observation in case of a possible concussion. I had been given a glass of water. At least it had ice in it.

"Witnesses." Belsen answered my question. "There were three witnesses to the attack, and they all independently agreed that at the last moment, the SUV swerved away from you and toward Mr. Rogers. Otherwise, you would have been a wet spot on the road."

"So they were just trying to scare me?"

"Scare you? I guess you could say that," Detective Joiner said. "They wanted to make sure you know they aren't through looking for that painting. And that they can find you anywhere you might go and reach out and hurt you."

I shivered. "That isn't very reassuring."

"It's not meant to be," Belsen said. "It's meant to be the cold, hard truth."

"What my colleague is trying to tell you," Detective Joiner

said in a soothing tone, "is that as soon as you get the Rafferty back, you had better let us know, so we can take the painting off your hands."

"The FBI wants it, too," I pointed out.

"It was our case first," Belsen said in an aggrieved tone.

"My boss, Mr. Tompkins, also wants to put it in his vault at the bank."

"The painting doesn't belong to him," Belsen objected.

"We don't really know who it belongs to right now, do we?" I pointed out.

Belsen grunted in disgust, but her partner said, "Well, I'm sure that once the painting has resurfaced, all the law enforcement agencies involved, and those who have some other proprietary interest in the picture, will work out a suitable plan."

Right, I thought.

Suddenly I felt tired, weak, and frightened. I wanted someone strong to tell me everything was going to be all right; someone who would hold me and care for me. I was tired of fighting everything alone.

My weariness must have showed on my face, because Joiner asked me if I was okay to drive. I told him I was, but he had an officer take me to my car and then follow me home. I waved to the officer as he drove away, feeling a sudden surge of loneliness. Slowly, I trudged up the outside stairs to my condo. I unlocked the front door and stepped inside, automatically flipping the switch that turned on the table lamp in the corner. Nothing happened.

"Laura, come in and close the door."

"Brew?"

"No lights until you draw the front drape."

I closed the drapes and turned on the lamp by hand.

Brew stood there wearing a pair of weathered jeans and no shirt. His body was lean and hard, marred only by a scar that ran down the center of his abdomen and around his back. I stared at him and felt my loneliness disappear.

"Do you know where the Rafferty is?" I asked.

"Of course."

"I need it back."

"You can have it any time you want. Do you want me to get it now?"

I shook my head. "I have something else I want to do right now."

I walked over to him and put my hands behind his head and pulled his mouth forward onto mine. Afterward, I grabbed his hand and led him into my bedroom.

"Do you think this is a good idea?" he asked.

"We'll talk about it tomorrow," I replied, kicking my bedroom door closed behind us.

When I woke up the next morning, I was staring at something I couldn't figure out. It was a design tattooed on Brew's upper shoulder. One reason I couldn't figure it out was because I was so close, my face was almost pressed into it. I shifted back to get some perspective, but like so many things about Brew, the tat still didn't appear clear. Brew slept on his stomach, facing away from me, so I quietly got out of bed and padded across the room, grabbing my robe off the door hook. I quietly left the room and went into the kitchen, where I put on the coffee. A few minutes later Brew came into the kitchen wearing pants and no shirt.

"Good morning," I said.

"Morning."

"Do you still like your eggs sunny side up?"

"Still do."

I pulled out my frying pan and got the eggs out of the refrigerator. This reminded me of all the times Larry had stayed over with me in my apartment during our senior year. Somehow breakfast together seemed even more intimate than what had happened last night. I glanced over my shoulder at Brew and saw a softness in his face that told me he was remembering the past as well. I put some butter in the frying pan and listened as it began to pop and sizzle.

"About last night," I began, staring at the eggs as if I'd never seen such a perfect shape.

"You don't have to explain, Laura. I was there."

"Where?"

"Outside the restaurant last night."

"You were following me?"

"Just to make sure you were safe. Not that I was much help. When they finally made their move, they were too quick for me to stop them."

A thought came to me. "Were you following me for a while before you came by to say hello? There were times when I felt I was being watched, but didn't see anyone."

"Yeah."

"That wasn't very nice."

"I wanted to make sure you weren't seriously seeing anyone. I didn't want my dropping in to screw up your life."

I thought about that for a moment as I broke the eggs into the frying pan.

"But about last night," I started again.

"Yeah. Like I said, I saw what happened. I knew how you'd feel when you got home."

"Frightened and scared."

"But also glad to be alive and wanting to prove it."

"So you figured it would be a good time to be here waiting for me."

He grinned. "Sure, there was some self-interest involved, but I also wanted to be there for you when you needed me. The way I see it, we both profited."

I thought for a moment, then nodded at the truth of his comment. I slotted a couple of pieces of bread in the toaster.

"I know it didn't mean anything more," Brew said. "You haven't been thinking about me the way I've been thinking about you."

I started to say something, but he raised a hand.

"No sense talking about it. That's just the way things are."

I slid the eggs out onto our plates and grabbed the bread from the toaster. I got the butter and some jelly out of the fridge, and put everything on the table. I poured more coffee for both of us and motioned for Brew to sit down. We sat across from each other, eating our breakfast in silence for several minutes.

"Where's all your gear?" I finally asked. "I didn't see it in the spare room."

"I divided it up into a couple of lockers down at the bus station."

"Why didn't you stay here?"

"I figured that once the word got out that I had the painting, it would be better if I wasn't around."

"Didn't you figure they'd think I knew where you were and try to beat it out of me?"

"I was watching you all the time. I wouldn't have let that happen. But I never figured they'd try to kill you. How is that going to help them get that picture?"

I shrugged. "Probably they were just trying to scare me, or maybe they're just crazy."

"But whoever they work for isn't."

"This whole thing is a lot more complicated than we thought at first. Did you see the two people dressed in business suits who came into the gallery yesterday evening?"

"I thought they were more cops."

"FBI."

Brew raised an eyebrow, and I told him the story.

"So you want the picture back?" he asked after thinking about what I had said for a couple of moments.

"Using it to set a trap seems to be the only way to capture the people who killed Peabody. Plus, it should stop them from visiting me in my home. Can you get the picture for me?"

"It was never really far away. Follow me."

Brew got to his feet and went out the front door of the condo. He walked along the balcony that extends along the entire floor of the complex. He walked to the end where the railing ended at a newel post. He glanced around to make sure no one was watching us, then flipped a knife out of his pocket and extended the blade. With an efficient gesture, he pried off the cap of the post.

"These things are almost always loose."

"It's in there?"

Brew slid out the rolled-up canvas. "I ditched the frame. It made the thing too awkward to hide. If you want the frame back, I hid it behind a big bush in back of your building."

I took the rolled-up painting into my apartment. Once inside, I unrolled the picture on my kitchen counter. It looked as good as new.

"Everything okay?" Brew asked.

"Fine," I replied. "Why did you borrow my car if you were going to hide the painting right here?"

"Just a little misdirection."

"You didn't trust me?"

"I didn't trust the people you'd tell."

He had a point there.

Brew studied the painting.

"It's kind of interesting. I never really looked at it before."

I nodded, thinking back to a time when Larry, the art student, would never have missed a chance to analyze an original work of art.

"This guy Rafferty has talent. I hope he's still alive," Brew said.

"I hope so, too."

Brew rolled the picture up again and handed it to me.

"Thanks for keeping it safe," I said.

"You're welcome."

I reached out and ran my index finger along the scar that bisected his abdomen.

"How did you get that?"

"I zigged when I should have zagged." His face closed up, and I knew he didn't want to answer any more questions.

He left the kitchen, and when he returned he had his shirt on.

"I'm heading out," he announced.

"You could always stay here."

He looked at me solemnly. "I don't think that would be good for either one of us."

"But you're not leaving town."

He shook his head. "Not without telling you."

I walked over to him and gave him a kiss on the cheek.

"Thanks for last night."

He grinned, and I could almost see the boy I knew in college.

"It was my pleasure."

As I watched him walk out the door, I suddenly felt very alone.

CHAPTER 21

After Brew left, I went outside and took a little walk around the entire condominium building, taking a long glance up and down the street. I saw no sign of a black SUV. I went around to the back of the building and retrieved the picture frame from right where Brew had said it was, behind a large rhododendron. I didn't know if anyone really cared about the frame, but at least this way it would be possible to restore the painting to its original condition. I stashed the frame in the trunk of my car.

Once back in my apartment, I took the rolled-up painting and slipped it in the sleeve of a lightweight jacket that I planned to carry with me. I doubted anyone was going to wonder why I was carrying a jacket on a day that was clearly going to hit the eighties. With the jacket over my arm and the painting inside, I walked out the door and down to the parking lot behind the building. I got into the car and drove off to work, much relieved that I would be returning the Rafferty.

When I got to work, I couldn't find a space behind the building because a couple of vans with the name of an alarm company were taking up the spaces there. I ended up parking a half-block away. I felt a little conspicuous lugging a picture frame and my jacket all the way up to the front door of the gallery. As I entered, aside from seeing three workmen at various locations around the room, I also saw Miranda and Mr. Tompkins talking in the back room. I walked over to them and put the frame and the rolled-up painting down on our worktable.

"There's the Rafferty," I said.

Mr. Tompkins glanced at the empty frame, perplexed. I unrolled the painting on the table.

"Brew took it out of the frame to make it easier to hide," I explained.

"I hope your friend hasn't done any damage to the painting," Mr. Tompkins said.

He came over to the table and began to examine the Rafferty carefully.

"It looks undamaged," he concluded. "Once we remount it in the frame, no one will know about its journey. And it will be safe here now. This security system will cover all the doors and windows, and there will be a motion detector that we'll activate at night. Not only will an audible alarm go off, but there's a direct feed to the police department, which, as you know, is only three blocks away. The alarm company has even installed a panic button in case of emergencies," Mr. Tompkins said, pointing to a large red button on the wall with the word *emergency* written under it.

"I'm sure that will make me feel safer," Miranda said, giving me an encouraging look. I still felt unconvinced. "Where is Harold's painting?" she asked me.

"Gone somewhere, I hope, never to return," Mr. Tompkins said.

"I sold it yesterday afternoon."

Mr. Tompkins's eyebrows rose in surprise, and Miranda smiled in delight.

"A young family came in and decided it was just what they needed."

"Hard to believe anyone would think so about that thing," Mr. Tompkins said dryly.

"Harold will be so pleased," Miranda said. "I have to call him right away."

Before she could get out her cell phone, I added, "The FBI were also here yesterday."

"What did they want?" Mr. Tompkins asked, clearly concerned. "The only time I've had contact with them in the past was when they were looking for stolen art."

"That's not exactly the case this time," I said, and went on to explain about the supposed plot to buy up Raffertys and kill the artist.

Mr. Tompkins snorted. "What a preposterous idea. But what can you expect from an agency that basically exists to find conspiracies under every bed?"

I looked over at the table. "Where did this particular Rafferty happen to come from?" I asked.

"I got it from the owner of a gallery in New York who has handled a lot of Raffertys over the years directly from the artist. He thought I might have better luck selling it to the Philadelphia crowd over the summer. I have to split the commission with him."

"Well, the FBI would like to use it as bait in a trap to catch the killers of Mr. Peabody." I went on to give him some of the details.

"I can't allow that. I'm responsible for securing that picture until the rightful owners are found. Unless the FBI is willing to pay twenty-thousand dollars to Peabody's heirs if they lose that painting, they can forget it." Mr. Tompkins shook his head. "There's too much government interference in our lives as it is."

"You can work out the details with them."

"Well, at least the picture should be secure here," Miranda said brightly, trying to lighten the mood.

Tompkins nodded. "Yes. By the end of the day, it should be safe."

He went to talk to the person who seemed to be in charge of

the workmen. Miranda walked off with her cell phone to her ear. I figured she was calling Harold to break the good news.

I understood why Mr. Tompkins didn't want to risk the Rafferty, but I thought there should be some way to apprehend the killers of Mr. Peabody. And, although the painting was now safely back in the gallery, I would personally feel safer if Broken Nose and his partner were behind bars. Finally, if the FBI was right, I thought it was important to arrest the people involved in this racket in order to save Rafferty, if he wasn't already dead.

"Harold was beside himself with joy," Miranda said, virtually dancing across the room toward me.

"Well, there's something you have to know. I took what you told me seriously and sold it for eight hundred. So you're going to have to make up the difference to Harold."

"That's no problem. It's worth two hundred to me to have him happy. Now if I can only get him to go back to his smaller paintings. By the way, he said you should select something from the inventory he's got here to have as your own, a special commission, so to speak, for selling his big piece. He's really very grateful."

"Oh, he doesn't have to do that," I said.

"I know Harold. He'll insist."

"No, really, a thank you will be enough."

Miranda gave me an exasperated look. "You know Harold. Once he makes up his mind, nothing will change it."

I nodded and tried to reconcile myself to being the owner of a real Harold Krass. I was determined to try to find one without birds.

The morning went by uneventfully. Miranda stayed around, and the workers were in and out. Having so many people around gave me a sense of security. I didn't think the homicidal couple was going to try anything with so many potential witnesses about. A number of customers came into the gallery, too. Most were just looking, but Miranda sold a beach scene, not one by Harold, to a young couple. I sold a photograph of Safe Harbor with the Victorian houses covered with snow after one of the rare heavy snowfalls. The man who bought it said he was going to put it in his office where it would remind him of Safe Harbor during the winter.

When lunchtime rolled around, Angie and I met at our usual bench. The first thing she asked me was whether Mike was going to be able to double-date tonight. I was about to say "Of course," when I realized I hadn't called him today to find out how he was feeling after last night's adventure. I had to admit that Brew had sort of pushed Mike out of my mind.

"Call him right away and find out how he's doing," Angie insisted. I could tell she was shocked by what appeared to be my indifference.

After I got through to Mike, I asked him how he was feeling.

"I still have a sore spot where I hit my head, and my back feels kind of bruised. The doctor at the emergency room said I'll probably have some discomfort for a few days, but I should be fine. There was no evidence of a concussion or anything serious."

"Good. I have some more good news. The Rafferty has been returned to the gallery."

"How did that happen?" Mike asked.

I gave him an abbreviated version of meeting Brew and his returning of the painting.

"It wasn't damaged in any way?"

"Not in the least. Brew removed it from the frame, but we can easily remount it."

"Maybe now that it's back in the gallery, those two killers will leave you alone."

"I'm sure the FBI would like to use it as bait to lure them in, but I doubt they'll get Mr. Tompkins to go along with their plan."

"Too bad. I think it's a good plan."

"Angie wanted me to call to ask if you were still up for our double date tonight."

"I really don't think I should. The way I'm feeling right now, I wouldn't be very good company. Can we reschedule?"

I turned to Angie and asked her Mike's question.

"Sure. Stephen said he could come out either today or tomorrow. I'll just give him a call and reschedule."

I reported that to Mike, who said that he thought he'd be fine by tomorrow night.

"You know you really should pay a little more attention to him," Angie said when I hung up.

I took a bite of my sandwich. "What do you mean?"

"Well, he almost got killed last night, just because he was standing next to you. A lot of guys would see that as a good reason to head for the hills. Mike seems to be willing to hang in there, despite the risk to himself."

I gave her words some thought. "I guess you're right. I've been so focused on how much danger I'm in that I haven't really thought about Mike. He could have backed out of this couple-thing anywhere along the way."

"He must really care for you," Angie said.

"I suppose. Or else he just likes adventure."

Angie raised an eyebrow. "Now which do you think is more likely?"

I smiled. "Okay. I'll treat him better from now on."

"You should. He sure looks like a keeper to me."

I went back to work, giving serious thought to how I could be nicer to Mike. I realized that I had been taking him for granted, largely because I was focused on the threats to my life and my feelings for Brew. But I had to recognize that, whatever

143

my feelings toward Brew, he was of the past, whereas Mike could be my future.

The workmen were still there when I went back to the gallery after lunch, but in about the middle of the afternoon, the one in charge told me that they would be knocking off for the day now. He said the system would be up and running tomorrow morning. The only thing left to do was to give Mr. Tompkins his introductory run-through on the codes, and apparently Tompkins wouldn't be available until the next day. I suggested he show me the system so I could activate it, but he said that the owner really should be the first to be familiarized with it. Then it would be up to him as to whom else would be given the codes. I could see his point.

After the workmen left, several groups of tourists came into the gallery. They looked at the paintings on display and combed through our bins of posters, but I didn't sell anything. Then the weather changed, the sky got cloudy, I could hear thunder rumbling in the distance. Suddenly, there was a fierce downpour. People went scurrying in every direction, seeking shelter. I stood at the front window and watched the pedestrian mall empty out. Figuring there wouldn't be any customers for a while, I sat at my desk and began to read. Slowly my eyes started to close. I struggled, but soon I was asleep. Obviously my night with Brew had been less than fully restful.

The harsh ringing of the bell over the door woke me. My head jerked up and an automatic smile sprang to my face. An elderly woman stood in the doorway, awkwardly pushing her walker forward over the doorsill. She ignored me and began looking at the pictures on the far side of the room. She wore a long coat, which made her seem a bit overdressed for the warm day, and she had on white gloves like women used to wear back in the fifties. I wondered if she was a bag person who wore everything she owned. Bag person or not, I told myself, she could still like art, and she deserved the same consideration I'd give to any other potential patron. I got up and walked across the room.

"May I help you?" I asked.

She turned to me and put her left index finger to her lips as if indicating I should be quiet. Her eyes went down to the bag she had in the basket of her walker. Her hand went in the bag and came out holding a long thin blade.

She smiled as she saw recognition dawn on my face. Not saying a word, she jerked her head in the direction of the back room. I walked as slowly as possible, sure that nothing good was going to happen to me once we reached the back of the gallery. But there is only so much time that can be taken in walking twenty-five feet. Before long, I was standing next to our framing table.

"Here's the Rafferty," I said, taking the rolled-up canvas off the shelf and handing it to her. She looked at me as if the Rafferty was the last thing she cared about. She raised the knife, and I shrank back toward the wall behind me, at the same time reaching over to the work table for something to use to defend myself. Just as my hand curled around the handle of the small hammer we used to mount pictures in frames, the front door flew open with a loud ringing of the bell. Someone walked in the door carrying a large picture. The person held it on his right side so his vision of the room was blocked.

"Laura, can you help me here?" a voice I recognized as Harold's asked.

The woman took her eyes off me and glanced in the direction of Harold. At that moment, I swung the hammer in a high arc and brought it down on her left shoulder. That wasn't the arm holding the knife, but I figured the blow would hurt anyway. She turned to me, her face a mask of fury.

"Hey, what's going on here?" Harold shouted. He'd finally

put the picture down and was staring across the room at us.

I raised the hammer again, ready to strike at anything within reach. Although I could see she dearly hated to do it, the woman turned away from me and, abandoning her walker, she ran toward the front door. Instead of getting out of her way, Harold stood there with his painting in front of him as if it offered some kind of protection. As the woman charged toward him, he raised the pictured until it covered his chest.

I barely saw the blade move, she was so fast, but in an instant the picture was shredded. She made one final sweep with her knife and Harold spun away from her and fell to the floor on his side. With the doorway clear, she stepped over Harold and raced outside.

I hurried across the room. Harold was struggling to get to his feet.

"My painting! My painting!" he wailed, holding up his shredded canvas.

All I could see was that the arm holding the picture had been cut from wrist to elbow, and blood ran freely to the floor. Harold followed my eyes, and finally he saw his wound as well. Without hesitation, he ran over to the disconnected emergency button and pounded on it.

"Emergency! Emergency!" he yelled, then fainted in a heap on the floor.

I called nine-one-one, then turned Harold onto his back and elevated his feet above his heart, which I seemed to remember was a way to prevent shock. I was looking around for something to use as a tourniquet on his arm when, thankfully, the EMTs arrived and took over. I knew the police would follow them quickly, something I wasn't looking forward to. I spent the time before they arrived calling Miranda, giving her a brief synopsis of what had happened, and telling her to get over to the emergency room at the hospital.

I went into the washroom and got some paper towels to clean up Harold's blood from the floor. Then I just sat and waited.

CHAPTER 22

"You have more lives than a cat. Maybe two cats," Detective Belsen said, shaking her head as though she considered me a sad waste of multiple lives.

Detective Joiner, who seemed to be entranced by a painting of a gull sweeping over the waves, turned to me. "You say she was dressed as an old woman and using a walker?"

I pointed to the walker in the back room. "There it is. You can take it into evidence. It would be covered with fingerprints except that she wore gloves."

"Disposable gloves?" asked Belsen

"White going-to-church gloves," I replied. Belsen rolled her eyes.

"And how did Mr. Krass happen to get cut?" Joiner asked.

"He came in carrying that painting," I said, nodding toward the poor slashed canvas propped against the wall. "She decided to run, and he was in the way. She slashed the painting first and then him."

"Did he try to stop her?" Joiner asked.

"Not intentionally. He just happened to be in the way."

"How do you think the woman knew to come here the day before the alarm system was going to be finally installed?" Belsen said.

"I'm not sure she did know. After all, what would she have had to do differently once the alarm system was installed? She could still have come in as a customer and threatened me, just

148

like she did today."

"You would have had the panic button."

"I'd never have gotten to it. She was as close to me as I am to you, and as you can see by what she did to Harold, she isn't afraid to use that knife."

The front door of the gallery opened and Mr. Tompkins rushed in. Ignoring the detective, he hurried up to me.

"Miranda just called and said there's been a stabbing in the gallery. Her friend Harold was stabbed."

"That's right."

"It happened here on the premises? Not outside on the mall?" he asked hopefully.

"Right here."

"God," Tompkins said, dramatically putting a hand to his forehead. "I'll have to call my insurance company to see where I stand."

I thought his concern for Harold was truly touching.

"What's that?" he asked, pointing at the painting Harold had been carrying when he was attacked.

"Another one of Harold's large canvases."

"Thank God it was slashed."

Belsen and Joiner glanced at each other, and I suspected they shared my feelings about Tompkins's callous behavior.

"Mr. Tompkins," Joiner asked. "Who besides you and Ms. Magee knew that your security system wouldn't be going online until tomorrow?"

"Miranda knew. No one else, as far as I'm aware."

"The FBI has informed us that you turned down their offer to set a trap using the Rafferty as bait," Belsen said.

"It isn't mine to use in that way. It belongs to Mr. Peabody's family."

"But the FBI has even offered to compensate the family if anything should happen to the painting. What have you got to lose? These thieves are brazen enough to come into your store in daylight. It's only a matter of time before someone else gets hurt. You have to help us get these people off the street," Detective Belsen said.

She paused and took a deep breath. That was the longest speech I'd ever heard out of her.

Mr. Tompkins pursed his lips. "I'm sorry. But I'm only following the advice of my lawyer."

Detective Belsen squinted at him with disdain.

"Is the Rafferty still safe?" Tompkins asked me.

I nodded. "She never put a hand on it."

"Show me where it is. I'm taking it with me and putting it into a safe deposit box in my bank."

"Why didn't you do that in the first place, instead of bothering to install a security system?" asked Joiner.

"The attempt to steal the Rafferty has only made me more aware that there are many thousands of dollars of valuable art on these premises. It is foolish to leave them unprotected at night."

"Aren't you afraid of leaving here with that Rafferty, given there's a woman out there who would kill to get it?" asked Belsen.

"My bank is on the next block." Tompkins turned to me. "Put the picture in one of our shipping cylinders and bring it back to me."

I went into the back room. I wondered how long the painting would be in the bank before some deal was worked out with Peabody's heirs. I might well never see it again. I unrolled it one last time and studied it. Then I did as Tompkins had requested. I returned to the gallery and handed it to him.

"I'm sure, Laura, that you will have nothing more to worry about, now that this picture is off the premises."

"I hope not," I said.

Mr. Tompkins strode through door as though he hadn't a care in the world. Belsen and Joiner looked at each other.

"I guess we'll just follow him for a little bit and see that he makes it," Detective Joiner said.

He and Belsen exited the gallery, leaving me alone.

The rest of the afternoon was quiet enough, although I remained on edge. I kept expecting that any minute a little old lady would come shuffling through the door with a long knife. A few people did come in, but they were the normal run of tourists looking for some kind of beach art. I didn't sell anything. I was kind of hoping that one of Harold's paintings might sell. I thought a sale might cheer him up during his convalescence.

Shortly before my shift was due to end, Miranda entered the gallery through the back door. She looked a bit frazzled. There was a crease between her eyes that only develops when she's tired or stressed, and her hair, which was usually just so, hung around her face.

"How's Harold?" I asked.

She rolled her eyes. "Physically he's going to be fine, but they're keeping him overnight for observation. The cut was very long, but fortunately not very deep. The doctor said there didn't seem to be any nerve or ligament damage. He can move his fingers. So it seems that once the wound heals, he should be as good as new."

"Then what's wrong?"

"Mentally, he's a basket case. He can't get over seeing his canvas slashed. He keeps talking about it as if a friend was murdered. Do you think there's any chance it can be fixed?"

I pointed to the painting leaning against the worktable. The entire center of it blossomed outward in long fingers of slashed canvas.

"I suppose we could try gluing it back together, but I don't think it will ever be saleable."

"Have you ever done any art restoration?" Miranda asked, looking over the painting carefully.

"When I worked at the Museum of Fine Arts, I spent a few months filling in as a summer replacement in the restoration department, but I'm no expert."

"Would you give it a try? Even if it can never be sold, at least Harold wouldn't have to look at it like this."

"Okay. We may not be able to bring it back to life, but at least it will look like a well-preserved corpse. Is anything else bothering Harold?"

Miranda sighed. "He's convinced his arm will never heal well enough for him to paint again."

"But you said he'll be fine."

"And I heard the doctor tell him the same thing. But his arm is very stiff right now and covered with bandages, so I guess it's hard for him to believe it."

"Mobility will come in time," I assured her.

"I know. But I think the real problem is that Harold is suffering from post-traumatic stress. Being attacked so suddenly like that has left him frightened and on edge. He gets weepy over the least little thing. He's turning himself into an invalid."

"Maybe once he gets out of the hospital, you should arrange for him to get some therapy. I imagine they can do all sorts of things now to treat PTSD."

"Getting Harold into therapy will be a chore in itself."

"If you can convince him that without therapy he won't be able to paint, you should be able to get him to go."

Miranda nodded. "Of course, you're right. You seem to be able to see this whole thing so much more clearly than I can."

"That's only because you're emotionally involved. It's hard to have a rational perspective on things when they hit really close to home. Are you going to be okay to work this evening? I could stay and just get something to eat on the mall."

Miranda waved her hand in an effort to appear carefree. "No, you go home and get some rest. I'm sure this has been upsetting to you as well, although you seem to be handling it fine. I'm better off working than sitting at home fretting about Harold."

"At least you don't have to worry about the thieves returning. They've probably figured out that the painting would be removed after this afternoon's episode."

"I'll still jump every time I hear that bell," Miranda said.

"Well, if it starts to get to you, give me a call on my cell, and I'll come over to sit with you."

"That's really nice of you." Miranda leaned over and gave me a hug. "But I'm sure I'll be all right. Anyway, there will probably be plenty of people coming in and out."

I said goodbye and went out the back door to where my car was parked. As I drove home, I thought about poor Harold being traumatized by the knife attack. That got me thinking about Brew, and how much violence he must have seen during his multiple deployments in war zones.

Even if he was much tougher than Harold, and he was, the trauma still must have eventually worn him down. As damaged as he seemed to me sometimes, it was probably amazing that he wasn't much worse.

Then I got to thinking about whether I had any obligation to help Brew travel the road to recovery. Didn't a person owe at least that much to a former friend? But helping Brew seemed like I'd be embarking on a long and open-ended mission. I might owe something to Brew, but I certainly didn't owe him the rest of my life.

CHAPTER 23

After supper I decided that, instead of my usual run along the boardwalk, I'd go to the local gym and use their aerobic equipment and work out with weights. Most of my enthusiasm for exercise had started when I found out that my predecessor on the newspaper back home had been extremely obese.

Deciding I wasn't going to get fat from sitting in front of a computer most of the day, I joined a gym. I know a lot of people look upon exercise as something they strongly dislike, but do for their health. I actually enjoy exercising. I find going to the gym a pleasant variation in the day. Something I do for myself.

I walked from my condo along the road by the beach, enjoying the tang of salt air and the mellow late-day sun on the water. Then I swung back toward town, and in a few blocks I was at the small shopping mall where the gym was located. It wasn't a large gym. I'd heard it had been built on the site of a former pizzeria. The building was large for a pizzeria, but small for a gym.

Since I'd put on shorts and a tank top for the walk over, I didn't have to change in the tiny locker room that sometimes smelled of cheap deodorizer. Instead, I went right to the room with the aerobic equipment. I walked over to the wall with the elliptical trainers and was about to hop on one when a guy passed by and said hello to me.

I said hello back, and he stopped.

"I haven't seen you here for a while," he said.

I vaguely recognized him as someone who had said hello to me the last time I'd been there in the evening, about ten days ago. I make a point of not getting involved in conversations, especially with guys, at the gym. They can interfere with my workout, and if someone asks me out and I turn him down, it's awkward to return there again.

"Yeah, I work a lot at night," I said, and went to move past him.

"What kind of work do you do?" He was obviously intent on keeping the conversation going.

"I work in an art gallery on the mall."

"Which one?"

He seemed nice enough, and didn't look like a stalker. I laughed to myself; the way things had been going recently, he was the least of my problems.

"The Tompkins Gallery."

His eyebrows shot up.

"Is that place still open?"

"Why wouldn't it be?"

Suddenly, as if he realized he had said too much, he began to hem and haw.

"Look," I said. "I'd like to know why you think that the gallery shouldn't be open. I won't tell anyone what you tell me. Anyway, I don't even know your name." I used my most beguiling smile, as if knowing his name was one of my few goals in life.

He didn't fall for it. "Okay. I'm a vice president in charge of loans at one of the banks in town."

He paused to see if I was impressed. I tried to appear that way, although it seems to me that everyone in a bank who isn't a teller is a vice president of something.

"About six months ago Tompkins came to us trying to get a loan to keep the gallery open. Well, you know how tight banks are right now when it comes to giving loans, and all he had as collateral was the inventory of pictures and the old Steichman Estate."

"He owns the Steichman Estate?" I said. I had seen the rundown mansion a number of times during my walks through town and wondered why no one had restored it and turned it into a bed and breakfast.

"He owns it, but there's a large mortgage. Anyway, *we* decided—a committee makes the final decision on loans—that his business model just didn't seem viable. Income from the gallery had declined last year, and the mortgage he was trying to pay off on the Steichman property was draining his disposable income."

"So you turned him down?"

The man nodded. "*We* did," he said, trying to emphasize that denying Tompkins the loan was a joint decision.

"Then how come the gallery is still going strong?"

"Maybe another bank looked upon his request more favorably or he found a different source of financing."

I nodded. "Thanks for telling me."

"Look, you can't tell anyone you know about this. If the knowledge was ever traced back to me, I could lose my job."

"Don't worry. I'm not a gossip. No one will ever find out where I heard about Tompkins and his loan."

"Promise."

"I promise." I even made a little sign of crossing my heart.

Still looking worried, he hurried across the gym and out the door. As I worked out, I tried to piece together what I had learned.

Mr. Tompkins was apparently short of money, and the bank had turned him down for a loan. He also owned one of the largest historic properties in Safe Harbor, but was carrying a big mortgage on it. What if, after failing to get a loan from a legal source, Tompkins had gone to an illegal one, some kind of a loan shark? And maybe there was some connection between this loan shark and the people trying to steal the Rafferty. That might explain why Tompkins was so reluctant to help the FBI capture the thieves.

Such thinking was a bit of a leap, but it made sense, I thought, as I hopped off the elliptical trainer and headed for the exercise bike. But I couldn't see how I could find out any more about the subject. As long as the Rafferty stayed in Tompkins's safe deposit box, nothing more was going to happen. In a way, I was just as happy about that, although I was still curious who was behind the attempt to kill Rafferty.

An hour later, the phone was ringing as I entered my condo. I answered and it was my mom.

"Hello, dear. How are things going in Safe Harbor? Do you like your job?"

This was one of those times when vagueness, to the point of lying, seemed necessary

"I'm fine, Mom. And the job is proving to be very interesting," I said.

"Are you making any money?"

"Yes. Actually this has been quite a good week."

My mother paused. "Working on commission can be difficult," she said, as if she didn't believe I was earning enough to survive.

"So true."

"Well, I just wanted to let you know that your grandmother and Roger St. Clair have moved into your grandmother's house."

"That's what they were supposed to do. I'm surprised it took them this long."

"I guess they felt some renovations had to be done, so it took them longer than expected."

"I see."

"Well, now that you don't have a place to stay in Ravensford, your father and I were thinking perhaps you'd like to come home and live with us."

No way on God's green earth, I wanted to say, but knew I had to be tactful. Living with my parents, especially my mother, would make every day a probe into what I planned to do with my life. Worse than that, the inquiries wouldn't be impartial because my mother had always regretted that I didn't become a teacher, as she was. And when she wasn't urging me to enter a life of pedagogy, she'd be trying to fix me up with the son of one of her friends. I knew I wasn't up to living through that kind of adversity.

"I'll have to think about it, Mom. After all, I do have a job on the *Chronicle*."

"As an *advice columnist*," she said in a way that made my job sound unsavory if not illegal.

"And more recently I've done some reporting."

"Is working on a small-town newspaper the way you want to spend the rest of your life?"

Now *there* was the question.

"I don't know, Mom."

The heartfelt honesty of my reply seemed to stop her in mid-tirade.

"You know I just want what's best for you, honey. I don't mean to badger you."

"Sure, Mom, I know it's just because you care. Oh, by the way, I've seen Larry."

"Larry? Oh, you mean Larry Stoddard."

"Yes. He called you, and you told him where I was."

"That was all right, wasn't it, dear? I always remember Larry as being such a nice boy, so polite and well mannered. Is he still the same way?"

"Pretty much. Of course, everyone changes over time."

"Is he still visiting you?" she asked, I think hopeful that he might be a potential son-in-law.

"He's around town visiting friends. I see him once in a while."

"Say hello to him for me and your father."

"Will do. Thanks for calling."

I hung up the phone and realized my ear actually hurt from pressing the receiver so hard against my head. If you really can get brain damage from cell phones, I'd be sure to get it from talking with my mother.

In one way, though, I knew she was right. I did have to make up my mind soon about what I planned to do after the summer. Dealing with thieves and murderers was a pleasant distraction, but eventually I had to get down to the serious business of what to do with my life.

CHAPTER 24

When I got to work the next morning, Miranda was already there. Her eyes had deep shadows under them, as if she hadn't gotten much sleep.

"How's Harold?"

"I called him right before I left. The doctor is letting him out of the hospital later this morning. I told him I'd bring him home, so maybe you could handle the gallery alone while I go get him. It shouldn't take long."

"Not a problem. How's he doing?"

"He's still convinced that he'll never paint again because of damage to his arm. The doctor still tells him he'll be fine, but Harold doesn't want to believe it. And he's more insistent than ever that you select one of his paintings as a gift for selling that big one."

"It *really* isn't necessary."

"That doesn't matter. If I have to listen to Harold go on about it one more time, I'm going to scream. Would you please do it now, so I can tell Harold which one you've chosen?"

Slowly I walked over to the local color side of the gallery and poked through Harold's offerings. Birds, birds and more birds covered his themes. Finally, I came across a medium-sized canvas of a canoe on the bank of a river with a view of the forest at twilight. I studied the canvas for signs of birds but could find nary a robin.

"This is my selection."

Miranda stood by my side and looked at it.

"That is different for Harold. I can't recall when he painted that. We've had it for a long time. Are you sure you don't want one of his more typical works?"

"No. I like the sense of quiet in this one."

"Okay. I'll let Harold know when I see him."

I went about cleaning and dusting the gallery, getting ready for the day, while Miranda was in the back cataloging some new paintings that had arrived yesterday. From nine to ten in the morning was usually pretty quiet because most of the tourists in Safe Harbor were late risers. Breakfast generally lasted until after nine, and it would be an hour after that before the crowd in the mall started to grow. When I was through cleaning, I went in the back where Miranda was just hanging up the phone.

"That was Harold. He's supposed to be released at ten o'clock, so I'll have to leave soon to get him."

"Fine. I'll hold down the fort."

"I hope we're busy today. The last couple of days have been kind of slow."

I nodded and thought about my conversation with the bank vice president.

"Have you ever gotten any sense that the gallery was in trouble financially?" I asked.

Miranda put down the inventory list and gave me a hard stare. "No, have you?"

"No. It just seems to me we don't do enough business to pay the overhead and keep two people employed, even if we are largely on commission."

Miranda seemed to relax when I had no new information to share. "Actually, business wasn't terrifically brisk last season. When I started here, things went flying out of the store and our inventory was much more varied. We had a lot of photographs of local sites, party games, various sorts of things. All that's

161

changed. I was even a little worried that Mr. Tompkins wouldn't open this season."

"I've heard he owns the Steichman Estate. That must have cost some money."

"He bought that the first year I was working here, when things were going well. I don't know if it cost all that much. The place is pretty rundown, and I think the owner was happy to unload it."

"Why did Mr. Tompkins buy it?"

"I think he hoped to renovate it and open the house for public tours. He even planned at one time to have the gallery moved to the old carriage house."

"But nothing ever came of it?"

"As far as I know, the renovations never got beyond the planning stage. It's a shame, too, because that house would really add something to the town."

"Maybe someday, when art begins to sell again."

Miranda smiled. "I'm afraid that house will be rubble before then. Well, I'm on my way to pick up Harold. Don't forget, the guy who installed the security system is supposed to be in at ten-thirty to show Mr. Tompkins how to arm and disarm the system."

After Miranda left the store, I sat at my usual desk and read some more of a book on renaissance art I had borrowed from the Safe Harbor Library. I was studying the set of beautiful color prints in the center of the book when the bell over the door rang, and in marched Mr. Tompkins, sandwiched between FBI Agents Spilker and Ganz. In his hand he carried a shipping tube. I got to my feet quickly.

"The man from the security company isn't here yet," I said to Tompkins.

"That doesn't matter," Agent Spilker said. Once again she was dressed in a black, or possibly navy blue, suit. "We're here on other business."

"Would you take the painting out of the tube please, Mr. Tompkins?" Ganz asked.

Tompkins's hands shook so badly, he struggled to open the tube and remove the painting. I took the tube from him and removed the painting myself.

"Is this the Rafferty?" I asked.

"Yes. We'd like you to remount it and display it in the gallery," Agent Ganz said.

I looked to Mr. Tompkins for confirmation.

"There's no issue for discussion here," Spilker said sharply. "We've got the permission of Peabody's next of kin to use the painting in a trap. His nephew was willing to do anything to help capture his uncle's killer."

"But surely Mr. Tompkins has to give permission for his gallery to be used," I said. He looked so forlorn that I felt sorry for him.

"Oh, but he has agreed," Spilker said with a humorless smile, "once we suggested that an investigation of his income tax returns might be in order."

Mr. Tompkins went over to my desk and sat down. His eyes were downcast, and he seemed determined to ignore the proceedings.

"But we do need to know if you and Miranda are willing to continue working here after we've set the trap," Agent Ganz said, looking into my eyes. "There should be little or no danger involved because we'll have the gallery under constant surveillance. But if you do refuse, we'll replace both of you with a couple of our own agents. We've just called Miranda, and she's agreed."

I thought about the sting operation for a moment. I certainly didn't want to relive the fear I had experienced yesterday. On the other hand, it would give me considerable satisfaction to

163

help catch the couple who had killed Mr. Peabody and tried to kill Mike and me. I also needed the income too much to take any time off.

"I'm willing to do it."

"Good for you," Ganz said, squeezing my arm. "As I said, we'll have people on the outside doing surveillance, and we'll have microphones inside the gallery everywhere but the washroom, so we know exactly what is going on. But remember, this is confidential, so don't tell anyone else about it."

"But how do you expect the thieves to know the painting is still here?" I asked.

"By the power of the media," said Spilker, opening the door. "And I think they are here now."

An attractive woman wearing a bright blouse and stylish skirt walked into the gallery. She was wearing so much makeup that not a wrinkle showed on her face. Behind her walked a short, squat man carrying a camera on his shoulder. The woman huddled in the corner with the two FBI agents for a moment, then came over to me.

She stuck out her hand and gave me a professional smile. "Hi, I'm Harriet Vance with Channel Twelve news. And you are Laura Magee?"

I nodded. I didn't always watch the local news, but she looked vaguely familiar. Probably because she looked like almost every other female reporter I'd ever seen.

"I'd like to ask you some questions about what happened here yesterday. Are you able to talk about what must have been a terrible ordeal for you?"

"I can talk about it," I assured her.

"Good." She smiled and moved closer, dropping her voice to a conspiratorial level. "They call me Dirty Harry around the station. Do you know why that is?"

I assured her I had no idea.

"Because I specialize in crime news, and several times—no, I'd say, many times, my reports have led to the apprehension of the bad guys. That's what I'm hoping to do here. Do you see where I'm going with this?"

"You tell the world the Rafferty painting is here, and when the FBI catches the crooks, you get to take some of the credit."

"Bingo. It's a pleasure to work with someone so quick on the uptake. Are you ready for us to start shooting? I don't think any of the questions are going to catch you by surprise. If they do, we can always edit."

Harriet stood next to me and shoved a microphone under my chin. The squat man turned on some bright lights and pointed the camera at me. For a second I froze, wondering if this was a good idea. Then, just as quickly, I relaxed and turned to face Harriet.

She turned to the camera and gave a brief summary of what had happened yesterday. Then she turned to me.

"Laura, what did you think when that woman pulled a knife on you?"

"I was frightened and surprised. I had thought she was an innocent older woman."

"But despite your surprise, you resisted her attack by striking her on the arm with a hammer."

"I was simply trying to defend myself with whatever was at hand."

"And you had the opportunity to do that because a valiant painter, Harold Krass, came into the gallery, interrupting the robbery in progress."

"Yes. I never would have been able to use the hammer if Harold hadn't distracted her."

"And Harold paid for it dearly. The hospital reports that he needed over thirty stitches to close a wound to his arm."

"Yes. And the woman destroyed one of his paintings as well."

Harriet looked confused by my little addition, but I knew Harold would appreciate it.

"And because of the heroic efforts of Harold and yourself, the thief ran away empty-handed. What in particular do you think the thief was here to steal?"

From off camera, Ganz shoved the rolled-up Rafferty into my hands.

"This painting," I said, waving the scroll like it was scripture.

"Could you unroll the painting and show it to us?"

Slowly I revealed the Rafferty. Harriet stared at it for a moment. I could see her wanting to ask if it was upside down. It wasn't. I had checked the arrows.

"So this picture that was the cause of so much turmoil is still safely housed in the Tompkins Gallery," she said loudly, just in case the thieves were deaf.

"That's right," I replied.

The camera swung around to focus solely on Harriet.

"So once again we can see," she said in confident tones, "that if people have the courage to stand up to crime, criminals will come away unsuccessful."

The lights went out, and the short man let the camera slide further back on his shoulder.

"Good job," Harriet said to me. "Too bad that painting isn't a bit more photogenic."

"Don't worry. The thieves will still want it," I said. "And that's what counts, isn't it?"

Harriet gave me a look as if she suspected me of putting her on; then she went off to talk with the FBI agents. I looked around for Mr. Tompkins and saw him in the rear of the store conferring with the man from the security company. They stood in front of the box that controlled the security system. The man was pushing a series of buttons on the screen and appeared to be earnestly explaining the virtues of the system.

I wondered where Mr. Tompkins was getting the money for such an expensive addition to the gallery. I thought it would be quite an irony if the folks who wanted to steal the Rafferty were paying to have the place made more secure.

"Just go about your day in your normal fashion," a voice whispered in my ear.

I turned and found myself almost nose to nose with Agent Ganz.

"I plan to," I said.

"Good. We have a technical team coming in this afternoon to install microphones, but we've already got surveillance in place. But we'd like you to sit down with one of our artists to develop a rendering of what those people look like. Could we set that up for this afternoon?"

"I'm off this afternoon. But I'll be back at four."

"Fine. We'll set it up for four-thirty." He took out his phone and tapped on the screen.

"Have you had any luck finding out what happened to Rafferty?" I asked.

He shook his head. "He hasn't returned home, and he hasn't contacted any of his friends or relatives as far as we know."

"So it's not looking good."

"No. Unless he got so frightened that he went into hiding. If he did that, he'll surface eventually. Otherwise we'll have to presume that he's dead. But we're not going to let the story out that he's missing until we've rolled up this gang. There's nothing they'd like better than for the art world to think Rafferty's deceased."

"How long can you keep his absence quiet?"

"Well, fortunately, Rafferty was a bit of a recluse. Not many folks in the art world outside his primary dealer in New York have ever met him. He tends to hide himself away when he's working."

167

"So he won't be missed right away."

"Exactly. People will think he's just busy painting."

"Laura, can I speak with you for a minute," Mr. Tompkins said, standing just off to the left of Agent Ganz.

"Remember what I said. You've got nothing to worry about," Ganz said, and he gave me a wink of encouragement and a cheerful thumbs-up.

"Do you know where Miranda is?" Mr. Tompkins asked. He was looking very anxious and pale. "Shouldn't she be here with you in the mornings?"

"She was in earlier but had to leave to bring Harold home from the hospital."

"Ah, yes, Harold. There's always Harold," Mr. Tompkins waved a hand in front of him. "But I shouldn't criticize the man. When I went to see him last night at the hospital, he promised not to sue."

"Would he have any grounds to sue?"

"There are always grounds. He might not win, but a lawsuit would cost me a fortune in legal fees. But you know what his only stipulation was?"

I shook my head.

"He wants me to carry at least one of his larger canvases in the gallery at all times. Can you imagine? A constant stream of those birding monstrosities."

Miranda hadn't mentioned Harold's little deal to me. I wondered if she even knew.

"What I would like for you to do is go to a Chamber of Commerce luncheon for me today. If Miranda isn't back by the time you have to leave, just close up the shop. The luncheon is at noon at the Harbor Side Hotel."

"What do I have to do?"

"Nothing, actually. Just be friendly and schmooze with the people. I'd go myself, but I'm not feeling up to it. The way the

FBI browbeat me into allowing this surveillance has left me feeling so violated, I only want to go home and rest."

"If I'm going to be leaving the gallery empty, maybe you'd better show me how the security system works."

Mr. Tompkins nodded and led me to the box by the back door. He showed me how you armed the system by pressing a button. That set the alarms at both the doors and the motion sensors around the room. He said I had two minutes of grace to get to the front door, get outside and lock the door before the system engaged.

"Now to disarm the system, you have to punch in the password," he said.

"Which is what?"

"Rafferty," he whispered.

I grinned. "Really."

"Well, it couldn't be something too obvious, like my name or a word closely associated with art. This seemed to work for me."

"So I just put Rafferty in and the system is disarmed."

"Yes. But you only have sixty seconds to do it, so don't delay. Otherwise you'll have the police here in a couple of minutes, and they won't be happy to be responding to a false alarm."

Mr. Tompkins turned and headed for the door.

"Are you leaving now?" I asked.

"Yes. I'm going home for a nap or a stiff drink. I'm not sure which or in what order."

After Mr. Tompkins left, the store was empty except for several tourists who were looking at the landscape art. I went over and talked with them for a few moments to see if I could be of any help.

I spent the rest of the morning working on Harold's damaged painting. Starting from the back, I used some canvas glue to re-attach the pieces, and then I flattened the canvas with a wooden roller. When I was through, the picture looked presentable, if not salable. There were faint lines where it had been torn, but Harold could always hang it in his own home as a memento. I looked at my watch and saw it was twenty to twelve.

Since no one was in the store, I quickly turned the sign to "closed." I left a note for Miranda in a conspicuous place, telling her where I had gone. Then I armed the alarm system, hurried to the front door, and locked it behind me.

I stood in front of the gallery for a moment, looking around. I knew I was being watched by the FBI. However, I didn't see a large suspicious panel truck or any people on corners in dark suits wearing earpieces. Everything looked perfectly normal.

Was that guy having an early ice cream one of the agents? What about the couple in shorts window-shopping across the way? How about that teenager with the skateboard? I decided that gaping at the crowd just made me look suspicious, so I headed off to the Harbor Side Hotel.

CHAPTER 25

The Harbor Side Hotel, as you might expect, was built right alongside the harbor that gave the town its name. Elegant in the fifties when it was built, it had been through a recent renovation that had brought it into the twenty-first century. It boasted a large ballroom, which could be divided by wall panels into separate conference rooms. And it was to one of these that the young woman at the desk directed me. The clock was just striking noon as I entered. About fifty people stood around in small groups chatting with each other. I stood there for a moment like one always does, feeling a bit overwhelmed at confronting a room full of strangers.

"Hi, there," a middle-aged woman said, coming up to me and touching my arm. "Is this your first time at one of these?"

I admitted it was.

"Well, first we have to get you a nametag. I'm Dianna Michaels, by the way," she said, sticking out her hand. "I'm the secretary for the group, which I guess makes me the official greeter."

She led me over to a table where lay a pile of blank nametags and a magic marker.

"Just fill one of those out and pin it on yourself. I know it's kind of tacky, but otherwise we'd never learn the names of new people. What business do you represent?"

"The Tompkins Gallery."

"Oh, George couldn't be with us today?"

"No, he was unavoidably detained."

"That's a shame. Some of the members really enjoy discussing art with him. Perhaps you can be his stand-in?"

"I'm sure I wouldn't be nearly as articulate."

By now I had myself appropriately identified. Dianna gave me a long onceover, as if checking to make sure I wasn't going to be lowering the standards of the group. I guess she found me satisfactory because she said, "Come with me," and led me across the room to where a group of five women were standing.

Dianna carefully introduced me to each member of the group, then quickly slipped away. Fortunately everyone was wearing their nametags, or I would have had no idea who anyone was thirty seconds after the introductions. A woman named Carol Meyer asked me what business I represented, and I told her.

"You've fallen in with the wrong group," she said, smiling. "We're all realtors. I'm not sure there's an artistic bone among us."

"Oh, I'm sure that's not true," a woman named Jodi objected. "I think we all have some artistic taste, or we wouldn't be able to sell houses."

"That's right," the woman next to me said. "A big part of the job is being able to take your client's taste and find something that matches it. That takes some knowledge of architecture and a good sense of interior design."

"And don't you hate it when you have a client with no imagination?" Carol said. "You show her an absolutely divine house, and she can't see past the paint on the walls or the worn carpeting. You have to keep telling her to ignore the cosmetic things and focus on the bones of the house."

"That's true in selling art as well," I said. "You sometimes have to train the buyer to know what to look for in a piece of art, especially if the piece isn't representational."

"When you say not representational, you mean it doesn't

look like anything?" asked a woman named Christine.

"Well, let's say it wasn't intended to be a photographic likeness of something. It might resemble an object in certain respects, but the artist has felt free to play with the appearance to make a point."

"I see," Christine said doubtfully.

"I think contemporary art goes very well in a contemporary house. It always looks odd to me when someone puts a traditional sofa picture over a contemporary piece of furniture. The two concepts fight with each other," Carol said. A couple of others nodded in agreement.

A woman behind the podium at the front of the room called us to order, and we headed toward our tables for lunch.

"It was nice to meet you," Carol said, walking beside me. "Although I have a self-interested reason for wanting to see George Tompkins."

"What's that?"

"George has been talking about selling the building where the gallery is located."

"I thought he rented."

"Most of the businesses are rented, but a long time ago, when real estate was cheap, George bought his building. I think he was hoping to sell it and then rent out the space for his gallery. I guess he needed the capital."

"How long ago did he discuss this with you?" I asked as we made our way to a table.

"Oh, I guess it must be over six months ago now. I've tried contacting George several times by phone, but he never returns my calls. Eventually I took the hint and decided he wasn't interested in pursuing the matter. I've been so busy lately that someone else in my office has been coming to these meetings, so I haven't seen George. I was hoping that today we'd be able to get together and determine once and for all if he's still interested. You wouldn't know by any chance, would you?"

"Afraid not. I have nothing to do with the upper-level business side of things."

"Don't feel bad. You're on the cutting edge in sales. If the gallery doesn't sell pictures, everything else falls apart. Am I right?"

I nodded, and wondered if that was what had been happening over time. But if things had been going downhill at the gallery, so much so that six months ago Mr. Tompkins had applied for a bank loan and thought about selling his building, what had changed to make the gallery more successful today? Or, if the gallery wasn't more successful, where had Mr. Tompkins gotten the money? Once again I was back to imagining him as part of a criminal conspiracy of some sort, one that might involve the Rafferty.

The meeting went on for about an hour and a half. After we ate lunch, there was a brief business meeting. Then came a speaker who talked about how to market your business most effectively. Since one of the few career choices I hadn't considered was starting my own business, most of his speech didn't relate to me, but it was interesting all the same. And I came away with an added admiration for those people who have the courage to start businesses of their own. I knew myself well enough to realize I liked the protection that comes from working in an organization owned by someone else, although that protection could turn out to be illusory. Just look at how I had been pink-slipped by the museum where I worked. At least when running your own business, you weren't at the mercy of the incompetence of others, and you had no one to blame but yourself.

After the meeting, I had some free time because I wasn't due back to work until four, so I went back home. After the fifteenth of June, the evening shift would be expanded from seven o'clock until nine. Every other day would be a ten-hour shift for either

Miranda or me, unless we got more help. Miranda had mentioned something about other people coming on board, but she hadn't alluded to the matter lately. I found myself wishing I knew more about how business really was at the gallery. I didn't want to work ten hours a day and go home with a pittance of a paycheck.

Once I was home, I put on the air conditioner to get rid of the mustiness in the apartment. Even though it was only the middle of June and the days had not been very warm, the humidity from living right across from the ocean could be intense. I changed out of my work clothes, poured myself a glass of water and flopped down on the living room couch to make some calls. First I called Angie to make sure she and Stephen were still on tonight for the movies.

"Hello." Angie's voice was barely above a whisper.

"Angie, is that you? This is Laura."

"Yeah, it's me," she continued whispering.

"Why are you whispering?"

"The boss lady read me the riot act about taking personal calls at work."

"I didn't know she had a problem with that."

"Well, I guess Stephen and I have been talking quite a lot on the phone."

"How often?"

"I guess three or four times a day. Maybe more."

I didn't say anything, but I could understand why Mrs. Mc-Crea might want to limit Angie's phone conversations. If I knew anything about Angie, she wasn't great at multitasking. If she was talking on the phone, she probably talked to the exclusion of everything else.

"Well, I just called to find out if you and Stephen were still on for the movie tonight."

"Sure. Stephen is coming out here directly from school, so he should arrive shortly after five. We'll catch a bite to eat then go directly to the cinema. You can meet us there."

"Don't rush. I have to work until seven. I'll have supper before I go to work, but by the time Mike picks me up and we get there, it will be close to seven-thirty."

"That's okay. There are a couple of shows starting around then."

After I hung up with Angie, I punched in Mike's number.

"Hello," he answered, sounding cautious.

"Hi, it's Laura."

"Oh, hi, Laura," he said, the warmth returning to his voice. "I was afraid somebody was calling to ask me to come back to work. How have you been?"

"Great. I'm just calling to see if we're still on for tonight." There was no response. "We were going to the movies with Angie and Stephen."

"Oh, sure. I just blanked out for a moment there."

"Not due to your head injury, I hope."

"Nope. The headache has gone away, and I feel fine."

"I have to work until seven. Do you want to pick me up? Or I can bring my car to work and then swing by to pick you up."

"No," he said firmly. "I'll pick you up at the gallery and we'll go in my car."

I wondered if Mike was one of those guys who always wanted to be in control. He hadn't given me that impression, but it was something I intended to watch out for.

"Okay. No problem."

"Anything else new?"

I filled him in on the attack at the gallery yesterday. After asking immediately whether I was okay, he listened carefully to my blow-by-blow description of the event.

"How did the woman know you had returned the painting to the gallery?" he asked.

"Maybe she just figured that I wouldn't keep it at home after they tried to steal it from me there."

"Could be. So Tompkins took the painting and put it in his safe deposit box?"

"For only a day," I said, and went on to describe how the FBI had virtually blackmailed him into allowing the painting back in the gallery.

"That's good," Mike said. "Maybe they actually will catch these thieves."

"Once they see on tonight's news that the painting is back in the gallery, it will be pretty hard for them to resist. By the way, this whole idea about an FBI trap is supposed to be confidential, so don't tell anyone. I probably shouldn't even have told you. Don't mention it tonight while we're out with Angie and Stephen. I love Angie, but she's a terrible gossip. If she finds something out, the world knows in short order."

Mike laughed. "Okay. They'll never hear it from me."

"So I'll see you at seven."

"Maybe I'll even come by a little bit early. I have the money to pay the rest of what I owe you on that picture."

"Wonderful. I'll get it packaged up for you."

"No need. I'll wait to take delivery closer to when I'm planning to leave."

My heart lurched. "Do you have a definite date when you have to go?"

"Not yet. And it looks like I may be able to stay for another week."

"Fine," I said, trying not to let him know how happy I was to hear that.

CHAPTER 26

After we hung up, I had a light supper of breakfast cereal and a banana. I figured that would hold me until we went out for something after the movie. I got dressed up in what I thought of as elegant casual: my best pair of khakis and a green silk blouse. I wore my white sandals, deciding that although Mr. Tompkins might consider them a trifle casual for work, what he didn't know wouldn't hurt him.

I got to the gallery a little before four and found Miranda pacing from one end of the room to the other.

"What's the matter?"

"Oh, Harold. What else? I just found out that he threatened to sue Mr. Tompkins unless he lets Harold put more of his giant paintings in the gallery."

I nodded. "Mr. Tompkins told me."

"Was he furious?"

"He was unhappy about it, but I wouldn't say he was furious. I think in a funny way he admired Harold for outmaneuvering him."

"Did he say anything about firing me?"

"No, of course not."

"There's no *of course* about it. I was the one who got Harold's work in here last season. He's here on my recommendation. If he starts trouble, it will look bad for me."

"I think Mr. Tompkins is taking Harold's threat pretty much in stride. I'm sure he won't fire you, for the same reason he won't toss Harold out of the gallery: the fear of a lawsuit. So I think you are pretty safe."

Miranda sighed. "I certainly hope so. Jobs aren't that easy to find, and I've been doing pretty well here."

"I thought business hasn't been as good recently."

Miranda hesitated. "No. But I got a nice increase in my salary at the start of this season, so even if commissions are a little off, I'm still doing pretty well. That's why I don't want to undermine Mr. Tompkins's faith in me."

So, I thought, another indication that Mr. Tompkins had come into some money recently.

"Why don't you go home and get some rest? You look worn out."

"I'd like to, but I have to spend the evening with Harold. I guess his arm is making him uncomfortable, and he's also on edge because he isn't painting. Painting is like therapy for Harold. It keeps him on an even keel."

"Has the doctor told him not to paint?"

"For a few days. Anyhow, his arm is so stiff, he can't extend it all the way. Hopefully, once he gets the stitches out and starts on some therapy, he'll be able to get back to painting."

"When will that be?"

"Not for another week." Miranda rolled her eyes. "Another week of hell." She picked up her bag and keys and headed for the door. "How was the Chamber of Commerce luncheon?"

"Interesting, if you have your own business."

"Someday I'd like to have a gallery of my own."

"Really?"

"Oh, I don't actually know anything about real art. But a place like this I could run."

"Maybe someday you'll get your chance."

"Not while Mr. Tompkins is around. He'd never sell."

Don't be too sure, I thought.

"By the way, the FBI were around this afternoon and set up microphones everywhere but in the washroom."

"So I'll watch what I say."

"Do you know how to set the alarm?" Miranda asked.

I assured her that I did, and with a wave, she rushed out the front door.

The hour from four to five was pretty busy. People in shorts and t-shirts came through in a steady stream, and I sold two small bird pictures, one of them by Harold. That would give Miranda something to cheer him up with tomorrow. People gradually began filtering out of the gallery around five, probably thinking about making reservations for dinner.

Finally, there was only one person left in the gallery. He was probably in his fifties, wearing dress pants and a long-sleeved shirt pulled out at the waistband as if he had been dressed in a suit and was trying to appear casual. He glanced around the shop and pretended to look surprised that there was no one else around but me.

I didn't believe his act for a moment. I figured he had out-waited everyone else for a chance to be alone with me. Call it paranoia, but I had good reason to be paranoid. Maybe the crazy couple had hired reinforcements. He sauntered toward me, and I edged nearer the panic button. When he was about an arm's length away, he reached in the pocket of his shirt and held a card out in front of him. "Sol March: Private Inquiries" it read.

"Is that like a private detective?" I asked.

His mouth pulled back over his teeth in what could have been a smile.

"They call it inquiries in England. I thought it sounded classier. Over there they call them inquiry agents. Doesn't that sound better than private detective?"

"A rose by any other name would smell as sweet."

"Huh?"

"Doesn't matter. How can I help you, Mr. March?"

"I'm trying to find a Mr. Mike Rogers, and I've been told you know him."

"That's right. I do know him."

The man took out a small spiral notebook like the ones Joiner and Belsen used.

"Can you tell me the last time you saw him?"

"Can you tell me what this is about first?"

The man paused with his pencil poised and appeared disappointed that I wasn't instantly forthcoming.

"Let's just say it's a little matter of an unpaid debt."

"He owes someone money, and they've sent you after him?"

"I wouldn't put it that way. But it is hard to collect from someone when you don't know where he is. Now where were we? Oh yes, when did you see him last?"

I was tempted to stonewall the guy. After all, I had no legal obligation to answer his questions. But I decided to give him whatever useless information I had because I suddenly realized that I had no idea where Mike lived.

"The day before yesterday."

"And where was that?"

"The Crippled Crow Inn."

"Is that here in town?"

"You don't know Safe Harbor?"

"Lady, I'm from Newark. This job is supposed to be a combination of business and pleasure. I get to go to the seaside and get paid for it."

"The Crippled Crow is here in town."

"That's the last time you saw him?"

"Correct."

"Is your relationship a romantic one?" he asked.

A good question from an inquiry agent, one I wished I had

the answer to.

"We're friends."

He nodded and seemed to smile to himself.

"How many times have you been in contact with Mr. Rogers?"

"I'm not sure. Four or five."

"In how long a period of time?"

"The last week."

"Where does he live?"

"I don't know."

"You don't know where he lives?" Sol gave me an incredulous smile.

"He told me he was staying here in Safe Harbor, but I never got an address."

Sol shook his head as if he would accept that answer for now but didn't really believe it. I didn't blame him. I could hardly believe myself that after all those dates with Mike I'd never pinned him down as to where he lived.

"When did he last contact you?"

"Today. We spoke on the phone."

"When are you going to see him again?"

"I don't know," I lied. I had reached the limit of truthful information I was willing to give out.

"You've seen him five times in the last week, and yet when you talked to him today you didn't set up a time for a date."

I shrugged. "I'm as surprised as you are. I guess he's just gone off me or something."

"I find that hard to believe," Sol said. "A lovely girl like you."

"Thank you."

The man folded up his little notebook and tucked it in his back pocket.

"You've been very helpful and I appreciate it. If you should talk to Mr. Rogers again soon, tell him that it would be in his best interest if he got in touch with me sooner rather than later.

Things will only go harder on him the longer he delays."

"If I should talk to him, I'll pass along your message."

"Thank you."

Mr. March gave me a little bow and left the gallery. I wondered what the FBI was going to make out of all that. I hoped they wouldn't start investigating Mike. Five minutes later a short, slight man carrying a laptop and appearing to be just out of high school came through the door. He looked around suspiciously.

"We're alone, right?"

"Right." For some reason, this was my day to have men want to be alone with me.

"I'm Agent Cummings. I'm supposed to work up composite pictures of the two thieves who tried to steal the painting."

"Okay."

He flipped open his laptop on my desk and took my seat. I pulled over a chair from across the room and sat down next to him, where I could see the screen. First he brought up a window that showed a number of different face shapes, and I had to pick the one that best fit our male suspect. Once we had done that we went on to all the other facial characteristics. In about twenty minutes I thought we had a decent representation of the man who had attacked me in my condo.

"There will probably be an easy way to recognize him," I said.

"How's that?"

"He'll probably have a large bandage over his nose. I think I broke it."

"How did that happen?" Agent Cummings asked.

"I hit him in the face with a lamp."

"Oh." He didn't say any more, but I thought he looked at me with newfound respect.

In another twenty minutes we had a good representation of

183

the woman. This one I thought was more accurate than the one of the man because I had seen her up close more frequently. Even with her attempt to make herself look like an old woman last time, a very clear image of her had impressed itself on my memory by fear.

When we were through, Agent Cummings saved the images to a file and closed up his laptop.

"We'll print up copies of these and have them distributed to all the agents who are keeping surveillance on the gallery."

"How long do you think this surveillance will keep up?"

He shrugged. "I'm afraid I don't know. That's a decision made higher up in the chain of command."

"I was just thinking that all this security must be pretty expensive."

"But it will be worth it if it allows us to roll up the gang planning to inflate the price of Raffertys."

"Still, it's only the work of one relatively minor artist."

"If they can do it with Rafferty, what's to say that the gang won't go on to do the same thing with other living artists?"

"I see your point."

Once Agent Cummings left the gallery, I immediately put in a call to Mike.

"I don't think you should pick me up at the gallery," I said, once he had gotten on the line.

"Why not?"

"There's a private detective looking for you, something about unpaid loans. He was here this afternoon, and I don't think he believed me when I said that I had no plans to see you again."

"Unpaid loans?" Mike said.

"That's what he claimed. Do you owe people money?"

There was a long silence. "I think I know what this is all about. I'll take care of it."

I wanted to ask more, but figured I'd let it go for now.

"Okay. But I'll bet this guy is out there somewhere right now watching the gallery, so unless you want him following us all night, we have to arrange another way to meet."

"What did you have in mind?"

"I'll leave by the back way and walk through the restaurant behind us. They know me there and won't mind if I leave by the kitchen door. Then I'll head down to the beach. You can pick me up on the corner of President and Beach. There's a shop on the corner. I'll be inside just out of sight. I'll run out when you stop."

"Sounds good."

When I was finished talking with Mike, I turned the sign from open to closed. It was a few minutes early, but I didn't want a last-minute customer coming into the shop and then hanging around, delaying my departure. I didn't know what the FBI would make of my sneaky exit, but they weren't supposed to be following me.

Right at seven o'clock I set the alarm and went out the front door. I darted around the side of the building and ran through the Mexican restaurant on the other side of the back parking lot, and up the alley to President Street. For the first time that day, no one had me under surveillance, and it felt good. Knowing that you're being watched, even if you can't see the watchers, is still an oppressive feeling.

I walked quickly down the tree-lined street. For the last half block there were no trees and I felt kind of exposed, but soon I reached the comforting shadows of the store, where I waited for Mike. I had one eye on the street and one on the t-shirts I was looking through when I saw the private detective drive down President Street. I took a large step back, so I couldn't be seen from the street. He drove past, then made a left turn and headed south on Beach. Either he was good, or I wasn't as clever as I thought I was. If he'd been five minutes earlier, I'd have been spotted. Two minutes later Mike pulled up. I ran out and hopped in his car.

"Any problems?" he asked.

I explained about my close call.

"No problem. We'll be heading north toward the cinema."

With that, he swung the car around and headed the opposite way on Beach from the detective.

After we'd been driving for about five minutes, I decided it was time to ask.

"Do you want to tell me about why you have a detective following you?"

"It's a long story."

I just stared at him. "We've got time."

"Well, it has to do with my work. You see, there was an operation that went wrong, and a person was left crippled. It wasn't completely the doctor's fault. It was a difficult procedure with this particular patient. Anyway, I was in the operating room at the time, and so the person suing the doctor wants to subpoena me. He wants me to testify that the doctor installed the artificial hip improperly."

"Did he?"

Mike shrugged. "It could have been done better, but it was a difficult insertion."

"Is that why you're on vacation, to avoid being subpoenaed?"

"The case is coming up next week, and my company really doesn't want me involved. It doesn't help our reputation to have our representatives testifying as to doctor error. It reflects badly on our devices."

"But don't you think you have an obligation to testify? I mean, this poor patient is probably crippled for life."

"No. He had a second surgery, and the problem was corrected. But you're right. I certainly would testify if it were up to me. However, if I showed up in that courtroom, that would be my last day on the job."

"But what if this detective finds you?"

"I guess I'll have to testify, but it won't be my fault."

"So why not let this detective find you? That way you can do the right thing and still keep your job."

"I can't just walk up to him and introduce myself. No, if he finds me, I'll accept it, but I'm not going to waltz up and surrender to him."

I didn't say any more, and we traveled in uncomfortable silence the rest of the way. When we pulled into the parking lot at the movies, I saw Angie and Stephen standing up by the door. Mike parked the car, and we walked to the theater.

Just as we were crossing to the front of the cinema, I heard the roaring of an engine down the road to my right. I turned and saw a dark shape coming toward me. I ran forward, jumped up on the curb and got behind one of the columns that supported the theater marquee. As I looked back I saw that the black SUV had swerved toward Mike, who had jumped up on one of the parked cars. The SUV hit the car, almost shaking Mike loose; then it tore away across the lot.

It probably would have made good its escape except for a car that came speeding down the road to the cinema and hit the SUV broadside, forcing it into a line of parked cars, where it came to a stop. Mike got off the hood of the car and raced across the parking lot toward the SUV. I took off after him. By the time I got there, he was trying to pull the driver out from behind the steering wheel.

"Who hired you?" Mike shouted, tugging on the man's shirt. The door wouldn't open more than partway, so he couldn't get the man out of the vehicle. It was the same person who had tried to steal the Rafferty, and I noted with some satisfaction that he had a bandage on his nose and both of his eyes were black.

"Talk to me or I'll break that nose again for you," Mike said, cocking his fist.

"No!" the man wailed.

"Then talk."

The man hesitated and I saw the uncertainty in his eyes. He opened his mouth just as Angie and Stephen ran up. Stephen was breathing heavily and was red in the face.

"Some people called nine-one-one," he said. "The police are on the way."

"Our friend here was about to tell us something," I said. But when I turned back to him his expression had changed to one of complete noncooperation.

"I'm not saying anything. I want a lawyer," he said sullenly.

I saw Mike's arm go back. I reached over and grabbed him.

"You don't want to be the one to go to jail, do you?"

For a long moment his body remained tense, and I thought he was going to strike the driver. Finally, he relaxed.

"Fine, we'll do it the legal way."

"Always best," Stephen said.

"Spoken like a true fifth-grade teacher," Mike snapped.

Stephen blushed but didn't say anything. Angie took his arm.

"You shouldn't say that," she said, glaring at Mike. "He was only looking out for your own good."

Mike stared hard at her for a moment, then he nodded.

"You're right. I apologize," he said to Stephen. He put out his hand and Stephen shook it.

"No problem," Stephen said. "If I were in your place, I'd have wanted to slug him myself."

Mike nodded and walked away from us with his head up, listening to sirens howling in the distance.

In a few minutes two uniformed officers arrived. They took our statements, and once we mentioned the connection to Mr. Peabody's death and the attack in my apartment, they put in a call to my favorite detective team of Belsen and Joiner. A tow truck arrived and moved the SUV far enough back that the driver could be extricated from the vehicle. He was immediately put in cuffs and arrested.

Two other officers got busy taking information from the irate motorists whose cars had been damaged. Belsen and Joiner arrived about forty minutes after the incident. By then no one was left in front of the theater except the four of us, and one officer who was probably there to make sure we didn't leave.

"Don't you guys ever get into any trouble during the day when we're not on duty?" Belsen asked.

Since this was about the friendliest greeting I'd ever received from her, I smiled.

"What makes you so happy, Ms. Magee?"

"That we've finally caught half of the team that's been terrorizing me."

"So what happened here?" Joiner asked.

"We already told the other officers," Mike said.

"Well that's good, because it means you should have all the facts together to tell us."

So each of us went through our version of events. Belsen and Joiner listened and took notes. They seemed particularly interested in how the SUV had swerved away from me and toward Mike.

"Did you know that guy?" Joiner asked Mike.

"Never saw him before."

"So he had no reason to want to hurt you?"

"I don't think he was specifically trying to hurt me. When he couldn't get to Laura, he just went toward the next target of opportunity."

Joiner seemed to consider that.

"Any idea how they knew you'd be here?" asked Belsen.

"I guess they must have followed me from the gallery," I said.

That's what I said, but I couldn't see how it could have happened. I'd sneaked out the back to give that detective the slip. It would have been almost impossible for the SUV guy to follow me from the gallery to here unless he was the greatest scout who had ever lived. I wasn't going to say anything to the cops about that, because I didn't want to tell them about Mike's problem with the private detective trying to subpoena him.

"Okay, I guess that's all for now," Joiner said, flipping his notebook closed.

"What about the FBI?" I asked.

Belsen grunted. "What about them?"

"Well, aren't you going to tell them that you've captured one of the guys they've been looking for?"

"Sure, we'll get around to it. Probably sometime in the wee hours of the morning after we've had a chance to interrogate the guy."

"He didn't seem very willing to talk," Stephen said.

Belsen gave him a look that suggested she had ways of getting people to talk.

"Let's go out to get something to eat," Stephen said once Belsen and Joiner had driven away. "It's too late for a movie, but food is always good."

"You can eat at a time like this?" I said.

"Sorry, it's the way I deal with stress."

"I wouldn't mind getting something, either," Angie said.

I looked over at Mike, who was staring at the ground, pre-occupied.

"Feel like getting something to eat?" I asked.

He shook his head. "Look, I've just remembered that there's something for work I have to do tonight. If you want to stay, that's fine, but I've got to get back."

"You can come with us," Angie said to me. "Stephen will take you home?"

Stephen nodded.

"I guess I'll go with Angie," I said.

"Okay." Mike replied, not looking as if it mattered to him either way. He seemed in a hurry to be gone.

"I'll call you tomorrow," I said, giving him a quick kiss on the cheek.

He nodded and headed back to his car.

"I wonder what that was all about," Angie said.

"He's just got some problems at work right now," I said.

We all piled into Stephen's compact car, and Angie gave him directions to a nearby coffee shop. Ten minutes later we were sitting in a booth. Stephen had ordered a piece of coconut custard pie, Angie had selected the chocolate cream again, and I asked for a bowl of Jell-O.

"Jell-O!" Angie said. "Live it up a little, Laura. You're skinny as a rail. A little pie won't hurt you."

"If I had a piece of pie I'd have to run an extra three miles to work off the calories," I said.

Angie shook her head. "You could use a little more meat on your bones."

I smiled to myself. That was what my father had always said when I was a little girl. And maybe that had been true when I was small, but following his advice had turned me into a rather plump twelve-year-old. Being overweight as a teen is very difficult. Along with all the normal social problems and the concerns about being unpopular, weight is just another issue to consider. So when I turned thirteen, I determined to lose weight. I became interested in sports, exercised regularly, and watched my diet. The results were gratifying, and the discipline carried over to my studies. I had drifted away from exercise during college and after, but now it felt good to be back in control again. I really had my act together, except when it came to the larger issue of what to do with my life.

The pies arrived at the table; eight-inch-thick slices that, I have to admit, looked delicious. I struggled to get the full enjoyment out of my Jell-O, which had a swirl of watery whipped cream on top that I thought about taking off but didn't.

"So I guess you'll be able to stay out here all the time, now that school is over?" I asked Stephen.

"Is school over?" Angie asked.

Stephen shook his head. "Not until the end of this week. Three more days to go."

"That's funny. There was a woman in the gallery from Philadelphia over the weekend who said her children had gotten out at the end of last week."

Stephen shrugged. "Maybe she just lives near Philly. All the local school districts have slightly different calendars."

"That must be it," I said, unconvinced. I wondered if Stephen was lying to Angie because he didn't want to tell her he was already living in Safe Harbor full time. If that was true, it didn't bode well for their relationship. Did he want to keep their dating to an occasional thing instead of running the risk of having her expect more of his time? If so, he had only bought himself a reprieve until the end of the week. Angie would certainly be expecting to see more of him starting then.

"Why would Mike be worried about work?" Angie asked.

I shrugged. "Something about a knee or hip that didn't work as well as the patient expected."

"Yeah," Stephen said "My Uncle Bill has an artificial knee. He has a lot less pain than before, but it doesn't work the same as a real knee. And he can't do all the running he used to do. The doctor told him the more he uses the knee, the sooner it will wear out."

"Your uncle was a runner?" I asked.

Stephen grinned. "Yeah, he's on the more active side of the family."

"Maybe when you're out here full time, we could go on walks together," Angie suggested.

"Don't you like me chubby?" Stephen asked, getting red in the face.

"Sure I do, but it can't be good for your health, and I could stand to lose a little weight."

"We'll see," Stephen said with a stubborn look on his face.

Angie reached over and patted the hand that wasn't scooping up coconut custard pie.

"Don't worry. I love you just the way you are."

Stephen nodded and gave a faint smile.

I thought Angie was rushing things a little. After all, she and Stephen had only been dating about a week, and she was already sounding like a wife. I knew Angie really wanted this relationship to work out, but charging in like that would only serve to frighten Stephen away.

"I wonder how that guy who tried to run us over knew where I'd be."

"Like you said earlier, he probably followed you from the gallery," Stephen said.

I shook my head. "I really paid attention to my surroundings when I left to meet Mike. I'd almost swear that no one was following me."

"Maybe he was following me," Angie said.

"You?" I asked.

"Sure. If these people have been watching you for a couple of weeks, they know we eat lunch together. They might have even been following us the other night when we went to the movies. So maybe they split up and one of them followed me tonight just to see if we were going to get together."

"That sounds plausible," Stephen said. "If these guys are as professional as the police and the FBI think, they would be smart enough to do that."

I nodded. It still seemed rather time-consuming to be following Angie on the off chance that we'd be getting together. But no other explanation made sense to me.

"I guess you're right," I said, finishing the last of my decaf coffee. I planned to have a good night's sleep. Stephen and Angie washed down the last of their pie with diet colas.

As we walked back to the car, Angie grabbed my arm and pulled me over to her side while Stephen went on a few steps ahead.

"I hope everything is all right with you and Mike. He seemed kind of odd tonight."

"Like I said, he's been having some problems with work." I paused, not sure how much to say. I thought about Mike's attitude toward the subpoena. "But to be honest, I'm not sure whether we have a future."

"Oh, no. Why not?"

"I guess you could call it a difference in point of view."

"Everybody sees things differently. Isn't that what compromise is all about?"

"Some things you just don't compromise on," I said, sounding self-righteous even to myself.

"What sorts of things?"

"Questions of values," I said.

I could tell Angie wanted to ask me more, but by then we had reached the car. Stephen had opened the doors for us and was standing by patiently.

"I have tomorrow off from the old witch. Tomorrow's your day off too, right?"

"Yeah, I'm off until the evening."

"I'll give you a call in the morning. We'll get together and talk some more," Angie whispered.

Since I didn't know how much I wanted to tell her about

Mike's affairs, I didn't respond. Sometimes having a girlfriend can be more of a problem than it's worth.

Chapter 27

Stephen let me off in front of my condominium complex and insisted on waiting until he saw me open my door. I waved down at him, and with a beep of the horn he and Angie were gone.

I went inside but before I could switch on the light. I heard Brew say, "Close the drapes first."

I dutifully pulled the drapes, then flipped the switch that turned on my one remaining table lamp in the living room. I made a mental note to myself that I should replace the one I used to break my attacker's nose.

I turned and looked at Brew. This time he was fully dressed. His brows were drawn together in concern, and he was shifting nervously from foot to foot.

"Where were you?" he asked anxiously.

"I went to the movies with some people."

"That guy Mike."

"He was there."

"I don't want you to see him anymore."

I was about to tell him he couldn't make decisions for me, but curiosity got the better of me.

"Why not?"

"There's something about him that I don't like."

"Can you be more specific?"

"I don't like his looks."

"That's not good enough, Brew. I'm not going to stop seeing

someone just because you have some vague dislike of him."

Brew slapped a fist in the palm of his hand.

"Are you off your medication?" I asked.

"I don't need medication to know a creep when I see one. And I didn't like the way you gave me the slip when you left the gallery today. What was that all about?"

"There were other people watching the gallery. I was giving them the slip."

"Yeah, a bunch of suits. I saw them. There were at least three or four."

"That's the FBI," I said, and told him about how the FBI had come to keep the gallery under surveillance.

"That painting is back in the gallery again," he said accusingly, as if it were all my fault.

"You know why it's there. It's a trap to capture the thieves, although already we caught one of them tonight." I told him about the car crash in the movie parking lot.

That seemed to make him even more upset, and he began pacing the length of the living room. I sat down and watched him, hoping he'd follow my example and settle somewhere. But he kept pacing; pacing and slapping his fist into his hand.

Finally, he stopped and turned toward me. "Don't you realize how dangerous it is when you give me the slip? Anything could have happened. You could have been killed."

"There is always a risk in life. And lately life's been a lot riskier than usual. But what can I do? We have to catch these guys trying to steal the Rafferty."

"Why do *you* have to do it?"

He had a point. I could always have let the FBI use one of their own to run the sting. Brew was right. There was something about me that enjoyed taking chances, especially when it involved a puzzle I wanted to figure out. If I had let the FBI replace me, I'd never know the outcome of the story.

"I guess because I like to. Why did you become a soldier?"

"For my country," he said in a raspy voice.

"That's not the only reason, is it? You wanted the excitement and the danger. That's why you didn't discuss it with me before you signed up. You were afraid I'd break the spell, and then you'd have to weigh giving up your art career against having a good time in the army."

"Good time. You think I had a good time?"

"Oh, I'm sure some of it was painful, probably pure hell. But a lot of it was good."

Brew stopped his pacing and leaned against the wall.

"You think I really could have had a career in painting?"

"You were the most talented of the bunch of us. All the professors thought so. Remember Professor Klein?"

Brew nodded.

"When he heard that you had joined the military, he said to me your choice was a great loss for the future of American art."

"I wasn't that good."

"Maybe not. But you didn't try to find out. Were you afraid that you'd fail? Is that why you went in the army, so you'd never have to find out if you just weren't good enough?"

Brew came off the wall and for an instant I thought he was going to hit me. But then he stopped and gave a small laugh.

"I'd forgotten how infuriating you could be."

"No, you haven't. That was what you loved about me. I made you see the truth about yourself. I would never have let you hide yourself away, just another cog in the machine."

"Maybe I could have been a good artist, but I was a good soldier. I'm not going to let you take that away from me."

"And I don't want to. But as good a soldier as you might have been, being a soldier wasn't as special as the kind of artist you could have become."

Brew turned and walked toward the door.

"Where are you going?"

He took my key out of his pocket and placed it on the table.

"I'm leaving now. You've got the police, the FBI and Mike to look after you now. You don't need me."

"Where will you go?"

He shrugged. "I've got a buddy out in Washington near Mt. Rainier. He's been after me for months to come out and visit him sometime. Maybe this is the time."

"You can't go on living like this," I said, standing up. "You've got to get help."

"I've had help. Now is the time for me to heal myself."

I walked toward him and put my arms around him.

"You can't do it alone."

Gently but firmly he disentangled himself. "If I can't, then that's the way it is. But I'm damned sure no one else can do it for me."

He gave me a nod and a small smile and then he was out the door. Much the same as when he left me eight years ago.

CHAPTER 28

The next morning I got up wishing I didn't have the day off. I was feeling down and disorganized, like I usually do when I think I've done something wrong.

In the light of day, my desire to be completely honest and truthful with Brew seemed like a terrible idea. He was obviously off his meds, and the last thing he needed was someone to remind him of what he had lost as a result of his questionable career choice. By telling him he had given up the opportunity to be a good, maybe a great, artist, in order to get high on violence, I was just rubbing his face in what he already knew. That was the type of hard home truth that people could barely handle when well. They certainly weren't ready for it when their minds were right on the edge or over it.

Angie called me as I was on my third cup of coffee. I was forcing myself to eat a couple of pieces of toast, so when I answered the phone my voice was indistinct.

"Laura, is that you?"

"Yeah," I said, after swallowing.

"Have you looked outside? It's a wonderful day out. The mid-eighties, low humidity, and the ocean temperature is almost seventy."

"Why the weather report?" I snapped.

"Well, somebody woke up a grouchy bear this morning."

I admit I smiled. Angie had the ability to do that to me.

"So on a nice day like this," Angie went on, "I was thinking we might as well go to the beach. You live right across the street, but how many times have you gone to the beach since you've lived there?"

"I haven't. I've walked on the beach; I've run on the beach; but as far as going on the beach in a bathing suit. I haven't done it yet."

"You do have a bathing suit, don't you?"

"Of course." I didn't think I had to share with her that it was the all-black type that competitive swimmers wear.

"So we'll do it the right way. I'll bring the beach umbrella and the cooler. Can you bring some sandwiches?"

"Wait, let me check."

I opened the refrigerator and looked inside. It was empty except for milk, a few condiments and a jar of mayonnaise. I opened my cupboard. It was equally empty except for a box of cereal and a can of tuna. Obviously all the commotion of the past few days had thrown my domestic side off balance. I pulled the loaf of bread off the table. It had at least six slices left.

"I can make tuna sandwiches. I'm afraid that's your first and second choice."

"No problem. I like tuna. I'll bring some sodas and pick up something for dessert at the bakery. I'll meet you at your place, and we'll head across the street."

I agreed and set to work making the tuna sandwiches. When that was done, I dug through my beach bag, which I'd never unpacked, and found my bathing suit. It had always fit me like a second skin, so I was surprised when I put it on this time to find it was rather loose. Since I didn't have a scale, I hadn't re-alized all the running I'd done must have taken off a few pounds.

When the bell rang, I pulled the door open to find Angie standing there, barely balancing an umbrella and a cooler. She wore a t-shirt that said: Teachers Make the Grade.

"A gift from Stephen?" I asked.

She shook her head. "I found it and bought one for each of us. I thought it would be cute if we wore them together."

"I see."

She took a long look at my bathing suit.

"A little institutional. You look like a Ninja swimmer."

"A friend who used to swim competitively gave it to me."

"I suppose it fit you at one time."

"Probably three weeks ago. I think all the running I've been doing since I got here has made a difference."

"Trying to stay alive probably burns calories, too."

We packed everything in the cooler and made our way across the street. We bought our beach tags and walked through the sand. I followed Angie, who was moving along like a persistent camel.

"Can we stop any time soon?" I called out.

"I don't want to be in the middle of a crowd," she said.

I looked around me at the sparsely occupied beach and shrugged. Finally, we found a spot where almost no one had settled. We were within visual range of a lifeguard, which I thought was a good thing. We spread out a blanket, stuck the umbrella into the sand, and placed the cooler in the shade of the umbrella.

"Now we go in the water," Angie said, peeling off her t-shirt.

She was wearing a yellow two-piece that showed a considerable amount of Angie. If my suit was too large, hers had obviously been purchased when she was several pounds lighter.

"I know," she said, reading the expression on my face. "I've put on a few pounds in the last couple of weeks."

"It's because you're happy." And going out with a guy who eats like a horse, I thought, but didn't say.

She pulled at the roll of fat in her middle and shook her head.

"I don't want Stephen to think I'm trying to make him into

someone he isn't, but I can't go on eating the way he does."

"Don't, then. As long as you aren't trying to keep him from eating, what you eat is your own business."

"Yeah. It's just that food is something we like to share. Let's go in the water."

We gingerly made our way into the waves, which, after a few minutes of acclimation, didn't seen cold. We went farther out and body-surfed the waves coming in quite strongly. Even though I'm more of an orderly-laps-in-the-pool type, I had to admit that jumping up and down in the sand and the sun was fun for a change. After we returned to the blanket, we sat for a few minutes just gazing out at the horizon.

"What did you mean yesterday when you said that you and Mike have a disagreement over values?"

"If I tell you, you have to promise not to repeat it to anyone, even Stephen."

"I promise."

I told her the story of Sol the private inquiry agent. When I was done, she stared at me for a moment.

"That must have been scary when you thought that detective was looking for Mike to collect money. I mean, thinking he was some kind of financial deadbeat. That would certainly upset me if it happened with Stephen."

"But I didn't feel much better when he actually explained the situation to me. If that device was defective, he should be willing to testify."

"It could cost him his job."

"Nonetheless."

"Do you remember how you felt when the museum let you go?" Angie asked.

I flinched. "I felt like a total failure. I didn't know what I was going to do. If my grandmother hadn't taken me in and helped me get that job on the newspaper, I'd probably have ended up back living with my parents."

"That's probably the way Mike feels. If he loses that job, he doesn't know where or when he'll get another."

"Maybe I wasn't trying hard enough to see things his way, but I just felt so sorry for the man who was injured."

"But he's had a second surgery, and he's okay. This lawsuit is just about money."

I thought for a moment. "I see your point. Maybe I should give Mike the benefit of the doubt. Sometimes I can be a little bit too judgmental."

Angie suddenly grinned and bounced up and down on the blanket.

"Stephen and I have some plans."

My heart fell. Was I about to become the first person to know about their engagement? Even Angie, I thought, wouldn't get engaged to someone she'd only known for a week, would she?

"What are they?" I asked.

"Stephen and I are planning to take a four-day trip to Washington, D.C. Isn't that great?"

"That's wonderful," I said, letting out a relieved breath. "When are you going?"

"Next week after school lets out," Angie said.

Again I wondered why Stephen would lie about when school ended. Or was he lying? It was possible I was misunderstanding things.

"What do your parents think of Stephen?"

"My dad loves him. Stephen is actually pretty good with his hands, and Dad gets a real kick out of showing him what he's doing in his workshop. Mom likes him because he's such a gentlemen and kind of shy."

"So they won't mind about your going away together?"

Angie laughed. "Compared to some things I've gotten into in the past, this seems pretty tame."

"Why Washington?"

Angie stretched out on the blanket and smiled.

"It's Stephen's job to take a group of honor students from the elementary school on their class trip to Washington next spring. He just thought he should know something about the city before doing that. So we'll do all the touristy stuff while we're there. Is that conscientious or what?"

"Sounds like a lot of fun. Can you get the time off from work?"

Angie's face fell. "That's the only problem. You know that next week is really the official start of the season, and we're all expected to work lots of hours. Taking days off is really going to get me into trouble. It might even get me fired."

"So what are you going to do?"

"I'm going to ask for the time off, and if McCrea doesn't want to give it to me, then I'll quit. She doesn't like me anyway. I should be out looking for another job."

"Maybe so, but it's always better to look for your next job while you've still got one."

Angie sat up defiantly. "You've got to have priorities, and right now Stephen is my priority."

I nodded. "Well, at least wait a few days until you're sure that Stephen's plans are definite. You wouldn't want to quit and then not have a trip to go on."

"I can't wait much longer than the day after tomorrow. But I'll give him that long just in case something happens. Stephen is coming back to town on Thursday, so I can ask him then."

"That sounds like a plan," I said, smiling.

Not a great plan, or even a good one, but it was definitely a plan. Giving up a job for a man under the best of circumstances seemed a shaky proposition, but for a man you scarcely knew, it seemed foolhardy. But I figured there was nothing I could say to Angie that would change her mind. She would see any negative remarks from me as an attack on her relationship with Stephen, and that relationship she would fight to the death to maintain. I thought about the mistakes I'd made with men in my own life. And I knew some women a whole lot smarter than Angie or me who had done stupid things for men.

After we had lunch, we stayed on the beach for another hour, then I told her that I had to get home because I wanted to go out and buy some supplies for the week. I helped her carry the gear back to her car, which was parked on a side street behind my condo. Once she was on her way, I went upstairs and wrote up a list of things I needed.

I drove my car to the supermarket and stocked up on food. When I'd come to Safe Harbor, I had promised myself I would work on improving my cooking skills, but between working evenings and going out on occasion, I hadn't really started on the plan. Now, I determined, was the time to do it.

When I got back, I was sleepy from the water, sun and salt air, so I had a nice nap. After that I made a pasta salad for supper. In the evening I went for a run and turned in early. As I lay in bed, I felt the most relaxed I'd been for weeks. I was almost able to believe that everything to do with the Rafferty, Mike and Brew was going to work out in a way that would make me happy. With that nice thought in mind, I fell asleep.

CHAPTER 29

When I walked into the gallery the next morning, Miranda was pacing back and forth.

"Problems?" I asked.

She waved a hand.

"Harold again?"

Miranda smiled. "Not this time, for once. I'm upset with Mr. Tompkins."

"Why?"

"Next week we go on our seven-day-a-week schedule and stay open until nine o'clock at night. That means we need at least one more person. Actually, one more full-time person and a part-timer."

"Is that what you've had in the past?"

Miranda nodded. "Phyllis Parker, a friend of Mr. Tompkins, has been the third full-timer for the last few years. She doesn't really need the money. I think she does it mostly as a favor to Georgie, as she calls him. But this morning when I talked to Mr. Tompkins, I asked him when Phyllis would be starting, and he told me she wouldn't be able to work for us this year. Something about her having to help with her grandchildren. So I said that we had to hurry up and hire someone to replace her."

"What did he say?"

Miranda's eyes filled with tears. "He just about tore my head off. He said that two people could run the store if we only had one person here at a time. He said there isn't enough business that we need two people minding the store. That's just not true. Once July and August come around, you need two people here, especially at night."

"Did you tell him that?"

She nodded. "He said that if I didn't know how to make a work schedule, he'd find someone who could."

Miranda paused for a moment to compose herself. I decided it was time for me to tell her what I had heard about the prospects for the gallery. Not mentioning my friend, the bank vice-president, by name or rank, I told her about Tompkins's loan attempt and about his plans to sell the shop.

"I never knew any of this," Miranda said miserably.

"For some reason, the financial crisis passed about six months ago, and the gallery was able to remain open. But Mr. Tompkins's refusal to hire more help seems to indicate that the situation has changed for the worse again."

"I know what I'm going to do," Miranda said. "I'll get my resumé out there right away. There are plenty of other galleries in town, so if I act quickly enough, I may be able to get another position this season. I would recommend that you do the same."

"The thought of putting out a resumé and going for interviews doesn't have any appeal to me. If the gallery folds, I guess I'll just go back home and work at the newspaper again."

"You're lucky you've got a job to go back to," Miranda said.

I nodded, not sure I was lucky at all.

"I wonder how this FBI operation is going. It gives me the creeps to be around here and know I'm being watched every minute," Miranda said.

I told her about last night's capture of one of the thieves.

"Good. Maybe now the other one will leave town. Between Tompkins and the FBI, this place is driving me nuts."

The doorbell jangled, and the other source of Miranda's

distress walked into the gallery. I was impressed by how different Harold looked. Gone were the confused expression, the nervous, jumpy eye movements, and the generally odd demeanor. Harold's eyes were clear, his expression firm, and as much as I could tell through the beard, he was actually smiling.

"Hi, Laura," he said, coming over and giving me a solid hug with his good arm.

"How are you feeling, Harold?"

He was wearing a short-sleeved shirt, and his right arm was bandaged from wrist to elbow. But he was moving the arm freely and didn't seem to be experiencing any pain. In response to my question he waved his right arm in front of him.

"Feels better every day. It's still a bit stiff and sore in spots, but when the stitches come out in five more days, I'm sure it will be fine. It might take me a while to be able to stretch the arm out fully, but all that will come eventually."

"So you'll be able to paint with no problems?"

Harold grinned. "I already am."

"You are?" Miranda said.

He nodded. "I just started this morning. I don't have quite the control I'd like yet, but it will come. You know, for the first few days I couldn't paint at all. In fact, I didn't know if I'd ever be able to paint again. But I found that as I sat quietly, not painting, ideas began to rush in on me from all over. It was almost as though not being able to paint enabled me to think more about what I was going to paint. Before, I just painted constantly and everything was rather similar, but now I think that if I take time off once in a while, my painting will become deeper and richer."

I stared at Harold. I'd never heard him make this much sense.

"You seem like a new person."

He grinned. "I did a lot of soul searching last night. Coming face-to-face with death and surviving has given me a new approach to life. I'm determined to make the most I can out of my limited gift as an artist. I'm not just going to paint what sells, but I'm going to work on projects that are meaningful to me."

I glanced at Miranda, who was looking at Harold as if seeing him for the first time.

"That's wonderful, Harold," she said, sounding stunned.

"I stopped by to see if you'd be free to get a coffee with me, so we could talk for a few minutes," he said to Miranda.

"Go ahead," I urged her. "There's nothing here that I can't handle."

After they left the shop, I walked into the back to see if anything new had come in, but nothing seemed to have changed. I wondered if the lack of new acquisitions was another sign that Mr. Tompkins was planning to close the gallery. The front door opened and Agent Ganz entered the shop.

"Good morning," he said. Dark rings under his eyes showed he'd had a busy night.

"Hi. I guess you know by now that we caught one of the couple last night."

He nodded. "The Safe Harbor Police gave us a call at three in the morning after they were through questioning him. I've been up since then."

"Did you learn anything about who hired him?"

The agent shook his head. "He's keeping his mouth shut. Has no interest in making a deal, even in return for a reduced sentence. All we know is his name, Bernard Walker. And we only know that because he'd been arrested before for assault."

"Did he give you any information about his female sidekick?"

"No. But he's listed as being married to a Clarissa Walker. She isn't in the system, but I'm betting they work as a couple."

"So he's sure not going to help you catch her."

"I wouldn't count on it."

"Do you have any leads on who hired him?"

"Nothing at all. He has no past affiliations that we know about with anyone in the art world."

"Are you going to maintain surveillance on the gallery?"

"Yes. All we know about the gang right now is that they want the Rafferty. They might make another try at it, and we could catch someone who is more interested in talking. How are you and Miranda holding up?"

"Pretty well, considering we're living in a fishbowl and trying to avoid getting eaten by the bad guys."

"Don't worry. You're in the safest spot in Safe Harbor right here. I saw Harold and Miranda leave a few minutes ago. How's he doing?"

"Surprisingly well. Being wounded seems to have made a new man of him."

Ganz nodded. "That's the way it works sometimes."

I wondered if he spoke from experience.

"Well, take care of yourself, and we'll be in touch if there are any new developments."

Almost as soon as Ganz left the shop, my cell phone rang. It was my grandmother.

"It's great to hear your voice," I said. "It's been over a month since we've spoken."

"Good to hear you, too, dear. How are you enjoying your new job?"

"It's much more exciting than I thought it would be," I said. I wasn't going to worry Gran with the details. It would be less stressful to tell her everything after it was all over.

"That's wonderful. Spending the summer at the seaside is a real pleasure. I did it myself when I was a girl. I still have fond memories of those summers."

"I'm sure I'll remember this for a long time as well."

"The reason I called is that I know you talked to your mother, and she probably told you about Roger and me moving into the house. Knowing your mother, she probably used that as a ploy to convince you to move back in with her and your father. Am I on the right track here?"

"Pretty much."

"Well, I want you to know that it is true we've moved into the house. We've done some renovating as well to the kitchen and the bathrooms. Lord knows, they needed something done to them. They haven't been changed in thirty years or more. But we haven't touched your room."

"That's great," I said. At least I had a room to go back to.

"However, Roger plans to use it as a home office. Now that he's getting older, he might not go into the newspaper office as much, so he'd like to do more of his work from home."

"I see." My heart sank. I truly was going to be homeless. With what I was paid on the newspaper, the most I'd be able to afford was a tiny apartment. Maybe I could get a cat and become a true spinster.

"No, you don't see, not yet. Roger and I have signed the lease on a new condo just for you. We are letting you have it free for the first year. After that you're on your own, but Roger will be giving you a salary increase in the coming year if all goes well, so you'll be able to afford it. Roger would very much like you to continue working on the newspaper, and he sees this as a small incentive to encourage you to return."

"Please thank Roger for me," I said.

"You don't have to make your decision right this moment. In fact, you can take the rest of the summer to decide. And don't worry if you finally choose to do something else. We'll always be able to sell the condominium, probably at a profit, knowing how Roger does things."

"I have to admit, I'm up in the air right now. But I will definitely give your proposal serious consideration. Thanks very much for giving me such an attractive option."

"Think nothing of it, my dear. Roger and I would both like to have you near us, but we also realize that a freed bird has to fly."

I hung up the phone and wondered what I was going to do. I knew that moving back with my parents was not an option. I couldn't return to being the good daughter again, and I had no interest in taking up a career as a teacher. I hadn't the patience or the desire to fit into the educational mold. My life had been too odd and eclectic for me to adjust to "normal" patterns. I knew that Gran and Roger would give me much more latitude to be myself, and working on the newspaper had led to some exciting adventures. But even their gentle way of arranging my life seemed a bit manipulative. I really didn't want other people planning out my future for me.

So what did I want? I asked myself. In an odd sort of way I could see myself living like Brew. Traveling from place to place on whim, and not having any long-term plans or career goals. But Brew was mentally ill, and that was the only way he could live. If he were well, wouldn't he be wanting to settle down and start a family? He hadn't chosen his present lifestyle. Years of war had thrust it upon him.

What was my excuse? As usual I couldn't think of one.

CHAPTER 30

The rest of the day was remarkably uneventful. By that I mean it was the kind of day that was normal before all the trouble over the Rafferty started. People came into the gallery, looked through the stock; some asked questions, and a very small minority actually purchased something, usually one of the smaller posters.

During lunch with Angie, she was still full of talk about her upcoming trip to Washington. I tried not to say anything, even though I didn't think she was making the right decision in giving up her job for someone she'd only known a week. I guess I'd never win the romantic of the year award. But I kept my mouth shut on the principle that being a good friend sometimes means letting people make their own mistakes.

In the afternoon, business got really slow. I decided that would be a good time to call Mike and find out how he was doing after last night's adventure. The phone rang several times.

"Hello," a voice finally answered softly and hesitantly.

"Is that you, Mike?"

"Oh, hi, Laura. You're lucky to reach me. I've been letting most of my calls go to voicemail because they've been from my bosses at work."

"What do they want?"

"Mostly to find out if I've been subpoenaed yet. I think their new idea is that I should leave Safe Harbor before the detective catches up with me."

"Are you going to leave?"

"No. I don't think so."

"Good. But why not?"

I'd been expecting him to say something about not wanting to leave me. So I guess I am more of a romantic like Angie than I care to admit.

"I've still got some business to finish."

"What business is that?"

Mike laughed. "Oh, you know, the business of getting to know you better."

That sounded phony to me.

"Have the FBI been in touch with you?" I asked.

"No. Why should they?"

"No reason, I suppose. They probably only talked with me because I'm still under surveillance. They told me the man we caught last night is named Bernard Walker. But he didn't give the local police or the FBI any information on who hired him."

"So he's a dead end."

"The FBI thinks his wife is the woman working with him."

"Maybe if they can catch her, they'll both sing."

"Well, I'm still sitting here with the Rafferty, hoping someone will make a move."

"They're probably wise to the trap by now. They'll either give up on the painting or come up with a completely different plan to get it."

"You're probably right." I paused. "Would you be free to have dinner with me tonight? I felt bad that you had to leave early last night, and we didn't have much time to talk."

After yesterday's conversation with Angie, I had begun to realize that I should have been more understanding of Mike's predicament regarding the subpoena. I thought if we had more quiet time to talk about it, I could better express my opinion.

"Thanks, Laura. But I'm a little nervous about going out in

public right now. Somehow this guy has gotten hold of a picture of me."

"Well, why don't we have dinner at my place?"

"That sounds good, but can I take a rain check and make it tomorrow night? I think I might have to move again."

"This detective has really got you on the run."

"He's good at what he does. But it should only be a problem for a couple more days."

"Tomorrow night, then," I said.

"It's a date."

When Miranda came in to relieve me at four o'clock, she was like a new woman. She was singing to herself, and there was a lively spring in her step.

"You seem happy."

"I just spent the afternoon with Harold. He's a new man. He's happy and funny. He even drew some sketches of me."

"I didn't know Harold drew people. I thought he limited himself to birds."

"You know Harold is a college-trained artist."

"I wasn't aware of that."

"Most people aren't. They look at all his pictures of birds and think he's just a good Sunday artist picking up some money on the side. But Harold is extremely skilled and trained in all areas of art."

"Then how did he—"

"End up being a bird painter? Well, he was an art teacher in a public school system for a while, but then there were budget cutbacks and he lost his job. So he had to decide whether to give up art altogether and go into another line of work, or find some way to make art pay. Harold chose the second course of action. His paintings aren't only in this gallery. They're in several galleries up and down the Jersey shore. He makes a good living out of his art. But that doesn't mean his heart is always in it.

I'm sure there are a lot of times he'd rather do something other than bird pictures."

"Is he feeling more confident about doing that now?"

"I think so. Being hurt like that has made him more aware of his own mortality. I think he realizes his time is limited, and if he's ever going to be known for something other than bird paintings, he has to start now."

"And he's going to begin with a painting of you."

"Well, that one won't be for sale." Miranda blushed. "I'm not exactly fully clothed."

I smiled. "There are a lot of famous pictures of nudes. You might end up in an art gallery some day."

Miranda blushed some more, but I didn't think she was really unhappy at the idea.

"He won't be able to give up painting birds entirely. That's his bread-and-butter art, but I think he has the confidence now to try different things. To experiment and see what works out."

"Wish him my best," I said, gathering my gear together and heading out the door.

When I walked out on the mall, I found myself involuntarily smiling because I knew a number of sets of eyes were staring at me. I felt self-conscious and awkward as I walked toward the end of the mall and headed down the street that led to the beach.

I had an empty evening ahead of me. Angie was busy going over her clothes, trying to decide what to take to Washington, and Mike was hiding from the detective. So I was pretty much left to my own devices.

The first thing I did after getting home was change out of my work clothes and into jeans and a t-shirt. Then I whipped up some chicken piccata that I ate with rice and fresh green beans. After some ice cream for dessert, I watched the news, read for an hour or so and then went out for my evening run. There was a golden glow over the ocean as the sun made its way to the west. Lots of others were out running, and I noticed that there seemed to be more women than men. I didn't know if that meant women were becoming more concerned with the health of their bodies than men, or if we just worried more about how we looked in a bathing suit.

When I got back home I changed and showered. Then I sat on the small porch in front of my condo drinking lemonade and watching the ocean until it became almost too dark to see. I went inside and bagged up my garbage. I didn't want to leave chicken scraps in the kitchen overnight. We had to take our garbage and recyclables down to barrels in the rear of the parking lot. As I was walking back to the condo, I went past the row of cars where mine was parked. By the glow of the streetlights, I could see something lying against the front bumper of my car. I walked closer, thinking it was a couple of bags of garbage, but as I got nearer, it took the shape of a man. Could it be some drunk who'd collapsed in front of my car?

I bent over the figure and touched his shoulder.

"Hey, you. Time to move along," I said, trying to hide the nervousness in my voice.

The head rolled lifelessly in my direction, and I recognized Bernard Walker.

Joiner and Belsen were in my condominium with me. The FBI in the form of Ganz and Spilker were out back supervising the forensics team. I had finally stopped shaking. My first reaction after seeing Walker's face was to run back to the condominium. There I fumbled around with the phone, finally managing to punch in 911. A calm voice at the other end told me to stay where I was, and the police would be there shortly.

Following the drill that I had unfortunately become accustomed to lately, I greeted the uniformed officers who arrived first, answered their questions, then told them this was part of an ongoing homicide investigation, which brought my favorite team of city detectives.

"Why wasn't he in jail?" I asked as soon as I saw them.

"Because he made bail," Joiner said. "We don't know who posted the bond for him. A lawyer took care of it."

"So he can just waltz out of jail after killing Mr. Peabody and attacking me three times."

"He allegedly did all those things," Joiner said calmly. "That's our justice system."

"Well, I think it stinks," I said.

Joiner smiled. "Stand in line."

"Did you carry anything with you when you went down with the garbage?" Belsen asked me.

"The key so I could get back in."

"I was thinking of something you might use for personal protection: a hammer, a crowbar, maybe a length of pipe."

I smiled. "Even though things have been a little rough lately, I don't carry a weapon to take the garbage out. Although maybe I should, given what happened to Walker."

"You see," Belsen went on as if I hadn't spoken, "what I'm thinking is that you were carrying something like that. And from out of nowhere this Bernie Walker fellow jumped out at you, maybe angry and cursing. And I'm figuring that you, frightened and in the heat of the moment, whacked him alongside the head. And all of a sudden, before you know it, there he is dead on the ground in front of you."

"It didn't happen that way," I said, suddenly frightened. I was surprised to discover I was more afraid of being falsely accused of a crime than I had been of the criminals.

"No one would blame you if it did," Joiner said. "Probably it would be self-defense. After all, this Walker guy had already tried to kill you a couple of times. Who could blame you?"

"He was dead when I found him."

"Why would anyone kill Bernie and then dump him up against your car?" asked Belsen.

"How should I know? Maybe his employer was afraid he was going to talk, so he killed him and dumped the body here just to muddy the waters."

"That's a pretty complicated explanation," Belsen said. "I like mine better, it's simpler."

"But maybe mine is the truth. Didn't anyone see or hear anything out there?"

"Nope," Joiner said.

"Well, that proves my point," I said triumphantly. "If Bernie had come out yelling and threatening me, someone would have heard him. He was killed somewhere else and then quietly dumped in front of my car. The forensic folks can determine that for sure."

I thought my logic was incontrovertible, and I waited for the detectives to humbly admit they'd been wrong.

"People don't hear things all the time," Joiner said. "Either because they don't happen to or because they don't want to. All I can say is, you'd better plan on staying in town until this has been cleared up."

"Don't worry. The FBI probably wouldn't let me go even if I wanted to."

The door opened and Ganz and Spilker came in. Ganz looked at Joiner who just shook his head.

"Do I need to get a lawyer?" I asked.

"Do you think you need one?" Spilker asked, taking up the slack from Belsen.

"I do if I'm being railroaded on a murder charge."

Ganz jerked his head toward the door. Joiner and Belsen left, although the woman gave me a long backward glance as if disappointed that I wasn't coming with her in cuffs.

"Even if you had nothing to do with Walker's death," Ganz said, "you'd better be careful."

"Why? Are you going to arrest me anyway?"

"We aren't the ones you have to be afraid of. Remember, somewhere out there is Walker's wife, the one with the long knife, and she might not require quite as much proof as the police before deciding to mete out punishment to the person she thinks killed her husband."

I thought about that for a minute and started shaking again.

By the time the police left, it was after midnight. I had been having trouble keeping my eyes open while they were there, but once they left, I found myself to be extraordinarily alert and on edge. I lay in bed imagining that every passing creak and thump was Bernie's wife creeping into my room seeking revenge. I hadn't imagined my situation could get any worse, but now I realized how my limited imagination had been surpassed by reality.

CHAPTER 31

I awoke the next morning feeling as if I hadn't slept at all. I knew I had, because after I'd tossed and turned until three o'clock, it had suddenly become morning, although it was a gray one threatening rain. I realized that I needn't have worried about Mrs. Walker's revenge last night because she would probably not even know her husband was dead until today when the news appeared in the paper.

It might take her a little while to find out where the body had been discovered because she wasn't likely to go to the police asking questions. But there was no doubt in my mind that a skillful criminal would have all the details of Walker's death before the day was over. Then I would really have to worry. Not allowed to leave town and being hunted by a vengeful wife seemed a classic example of being between a rock and a hard place.

Not paying much attention to what I was eating, I shoveled in some cereal and drank some coffee. I dressed a little more casually than usual, wearing slacks instead of a dress or skirt. I didn't know if Mr. Tompkins would approve, but it sounded like the gallery was just about on its last legs anyway. Taking an umbrella, I walked into work, finding that the gray skies and humid air pretty much fit my mood.

When I got there, Miranda was sitting at a desk going through some papers.

"Invoices?" I asked.

She shook her head. "My resumé. After we talked yesterday, I got angrier and angrier. Here we are risking our lives, and Mr. Tompkins can't even hire us some help. It's sheer exploitation, and I'm not going to put up with it anymore. I talked it over with Harold, and he agreed. He said that even if Tompkins refuses to show Harold's work in the gallery anymore, it's worth it if I can get a better position."

"That's good of Harold."

"Yes, he really seems to be a changed man."

"I'm glad someone is benefiting from this," I said, and told her about finding Walker's body behind my condo.

Miranda stared at me, aghast. "That's terrible. And they don't want you to leave town, even though that crazy woman could be looking for you?"

"That's about the size of it."

"I can understand if you're too upset to work today. Take the day off. I'll cover for you."

"No. Here is about the only place that I feel safe. At least with the FBI watching me, I don't think I'll get knifed."

"I hadn't thought of that. Would you be willing to work the afternoon shift again today? Harold and I have something planned."

"More sketching," I said with a mischievous grin.

Miranda blushed. "No, this is more of a business plan. I don't want to talk about it until we've got it solidified."

"Sounds intriguing. Tell me about it when you can."

I launched into giving the gallery a good cleaning. I dusted all the framed pictures on display, mopped the tile floors, and even straightened up the back room so it was in some kind of order. Miranda looked on, speechless.

"Do you always go on a cleaning frenzy when you're afraid?"

"Afraid or nervous. There's nothing that grounds you more than cleaning. You have to pay attention to every little thing around you, and if you really do it in a thoughtful way, then your mind can't wander off and think about horrible things."

The morning moved along slowly. Around ten-thirty some customers wandered in. I gave them even more attention than usual to take my mind off icky things. Miranda and I chatted about trivial stuff. We even stood by the front window and played a game of spot the Fed. The game lost a little of its enjoyment when we realized there was no way we could tell if we were right or wrong.

Around noon Miranda left. I called Angie and asked if she'd be willing to eat in the gallery with me because I was covering for Miranda. Sounding somewhat down in the mouth, she agreed. I closed the gallery and walked four doors up to buy a sandwich, hoping I wasn't outside the FBI's range of surveillance. As I came out of the store, I met Angie, who was walking down with a salad and drink in hand.

"Is that a salad I see?"

"Seeing myself in that swimsuit yesterday told me I just have to lose a few pounds. Even if it doesn't matter to Stephen, it matters to me. I don't want to be a fatty."

I let us into the gallery and darted across the room to turn off the alarm.

"What happens if you don't get to the alarm in time?" Angie asked.

"According to Mr. Tompkins, a SWAT team will be here in minutes. I'm not so sure."

I carried a chair out from the back room, and Angie and I ate our sandwiches sitting at the desk. It might have looked a bit informal if anyone came into the gallery, but too bad. That's just the way things were going to be today. Angie ate her salad but didn't say much, not even a word about the much-anticipated trip to Washington. Finally, I asked her what was wrong.

"I got a call from Stephen this morning saying he won't be able to make it tonight."

"Did he say why?"

"Just that he had some family business he had to attend to."

"That doesn't seem unreasonable."

"I know. And it's the first time he's had to cancel one of our dates. But it gets me all nervous that he's changed his mind about me and doesn't want to see me anymore."

"I think you're overreacting."

She nodded, but clearly wasn't convinced. "It's happened to me that way before, where the guy never says it's all over, but he has an excuse for why he can't see me every time I call. It's almost like he can't bear to break the bad news all at once, so he spoons it out over time. That just makes it worse."

"That's happened to all of us. Men are afraid of a scene, so they'd rather let us find out by attrition. Did Stephen say when he would be out to see you?"

"He said he'd try to make it tomorrow. I hope he does. I need to get this trip to Washington thing set in the next couple of days, so I can tell them at work."

"You mean quit your job."

"If it comes to that," Angie said, but I thought she sounded a shade more doubtful than she had the other day.

I told Angie about finding the dead body behind my condo. Her eyes grew huge, and she stared at me.

"You've let me go on about my little problems when you found a dead body," Angie exclaimed. "And I can't believe that the police think you could have killed that guy, although I wouldn't blame you if you had."

"Well, I didn't. But now I'm afraid his wife will be out hunting for me."

"Yeah, that crazy woman with the knife is pretty scary. Why, she could come in here any minute and stab us both."

Angie didn't know about the FBI watching the gallery, and I wasn't about to tell her now.

"She'll probably wait to get me alone somewhere."

"Why don't you come stay with me at my parents' house? You could share my room until this all blows over."

The idea was tempting, but I knew if I accepted her offer, I would be putting Angie and her family in danger.

"Thanks anyway, Angie, but I'll just go home and keep my door locked. The police are on the trail of the woman. Now that they know who she is, they'll catch her sooner rather than later."

"Let's hope it's soon enough."

When we were through with lunch, Angie was reluctant to leave me alone in the store, but I assured her I had a panic button that would summon the local police within minutes if I needed them. I promised that at the first sight of the murderous woman, I would push the button and run out the back door.

After Angie left, I sat at the desk and tried to read. I wasn't afraid. After all, the FBI was right outside, but I didn't like sitting around, passively waiting for something to happen. I wanted to do something that would bring all of this drama to an end. My cell phone played its tune.

"Hello."

"Is this Laura Magee?" a muffled voice asked.

"Yes."

"Go back into the washroom."

"What?"

"Do as I say."

I walked back to the washroom.

"Are you there?"

"Yes."

"We've got Mike Rogers. If you want to see him alive again, you'll do what I say."

"Prove that you've got him," I demanded. I'd watched enough

television to know I should be cautious. The phone went silent for several moments.

"Hi, Laura," I heard Mike say.

"What happened? Are you all right?"

"Don't do what they say. They're going to kill me anyway," Mike said in a rush. There was a commotion on the other end of the line and then silence.

"Listen to me." The muffled voice was back on the line again. "We have no reason to kill anybody. We simply want the Rafferty. Bring it to us after work, and everyone goes home and gets a good night's sleep."

I thought about it. If I said no, they would hang up and Mike was dead. At least if I went along with them, there might be a chance of saving Mike somewhere down the line. I couldn't see any reason why they would want to kill him.

"How am I supposed to get it out of here?" I asked.

"Yes. You *are* being watched by the FBI, aren't you?" the voice said, obviously pleased to be telling me he knew about the trap. "I understand the picture is out of the frame, so hide it under your clothes if you have to. But get it out without being observed."

"Then what do I do?"

"You start walking north on Union Street. Somewhere along the way a van will pull over next to you, and you will get inside. The driver will bring you here. We will take the picture, and you and Mike can go free. Do you understand?"

"I understand."

"If you make any attempt to notify the FBI or the police, I'll know, and Mike will die."

"What about Bernie Walker's wife? Is she out to get me because she thinks I killed her husband?"

"Don't worry about her. She knows you didn't do it. Are you coming?"

"Okay. I'll be there."

The line went dead and I sat alone in the store staring at the mirror across the bathroom, which showed one pretty shaken woman. I didn't like anything about this plan, but I was afraid to tell the FBI or the police because the guy, whoever he was, seemed to know exactly what was going on. And I remembered reading that most cases of art theft never resulted in injuries. Art thieves were generally interested in money, not killing people. But then I thought of Bernie Walker slumped against the bumper of my car, and got butterflies in my stomach all over again.

I decided that approaching the matter in a hypothetical way would put off having to make a final decision. How would I get the painting out of the gallery if I did follow that man's orders?

I really didn't like the idea of putting the Rafferty under my clothes. Having to strip in some thieves' lair in order to hand over a painting would make me far too vulnerable. I looked at the coat rack and saw my umbrella hanging there. The FBI had seen me carry it in with me this morning, so they wouldn't be surprised to see me leave with it this afternoon.

I went into the back room and got the Rafferty. I unrolled it and carefully placed it down in the framework of my partially closed umbrella. Then I completely closed the umbrella and snapped it shut. I hoped it wouldn't do the Rafferty any harm to be tightly folded for a few hours. I hung my umbrella back on the rack, figuring it was safest to hide the painting in plain sight.

I might have been willing to walk into the thieves' lair, but I wasn't about to do it without telling someone where I was going. I took a piece of the gallery letterhead and wrote out exactly the directions I had been asked to follow. Then I sealed it in an envelope and wrote "Give to the FBI fifteen minutes after I leave," across the front.

I had just finished writing the note when the bell over the door jangled and a customer walked into the shop. The afternoon was actually very busy. I sold three posters and a painting, one of Harold's, so I knew he would be pleased. When Miranda came in shortly before four, I was actually standing in front of one of the contemporary pieces and pointing out its similarity to the work of a couple of famous living artists. I didn't make the sale, but the chance to talk about stuff that interested me helped pass the time. In fact, I was already running late. What would happen if I wasn't there right on time? Would they think I wasn't coming and kill Mike?

"I sold another one of Harold's pictures," I said to Miranda as I headed for the coat rack, my decision made.

"I'd like to talk about that business deal I mentioned to you this morning if you have the time."

"I'd love to talk about it, but I really have to leave. I promised to meet somebody."

Miranda smiled. "No problem. We'll discuss it in the morning."

I handed her the envelope. She read what was written on the front and opened her mouth to say something, but I put my finger to my lips. Before she could do anything more, I waved goodbye and rushed out the door. Immediately I forced myself to slow down and walk casually. Running off would surely lead to some FBI agent following me. I walked up Union Street, not going too fast or too slow, and pointing the way ahead with my umbrella. I had gone about five blocks and was starting to wonder if I was too late, when a van pulled up beside me. Sol March leaned out the driver's-side window.

"Get in the back, sweetheart," he called out.

Relief flooded over me. Sol might have been a lot of things, but he didn't impress me as a cold-blooded killer. I climbed in the back of the van.

"Are we going far?" I asked.

"Nah. Just a few blocks."

Sol drove up to the next corner and made a right turn. He traveled four more blocks, then pulled into a wide driveway in front of what I recognized as the Steichman Estate, the one that Mr. Tompkins supposedly owned. Not stopping at the front door, he pulled around the house and stopped in front of what appeared to be a carriage house. Sol got out of the van and indicated I should follow him. The inside of the building was so dark, for a moment everything was indistinct. I stumbled over some unevenness in the wood floor, and Sol grabbed my arm to steady me.

"What's this all about, Sol?" I whispered.

At first I thought he wasn't going to answer me. Then he bent down close to my ear.

"As near as I can figure out, this Mike guy owes the boss some money. The boss says that if he gets the painting from Mike then they'll call it square. You do have the painting, right?"

I held up the umbrella. "It's in here."

Sol took the umbrella in one hand and my arm in the other and led me across the open space. We went into a room defined by piled-up bales of hay. Mike lay on the floor; his hands were cuffed behind him around one of the barn posts. He looked up as I walked into the area.

"You shouldn't have come," he said to me in a hoarse voice.

"Don't be telling her that," Sol said. "She's doing you a big favor by bringing this painting to get you off the hook."

"I've been trying to tell you that they're going to kill me. Now they'll kill her, too."

"Nobody's going to get killed," Sol said. "But I'm afraid you are going to have to be cuffed for a while," he said to me.

"Why?"

"We have to wait here until the boss comes, and he doesn't

want anybody wandering away."

Sol helped me sit down next to a post about five feet away from Mike. He gently pulled my hands behind my back, and I felt metal cuffs tighten around my wrists.

"Not too tight, are they?" he asked.

"No," I said, thinking how silly it was to act as if being cuffed was just a normal part of any business conference.

Sol stood back and looked at the two of us.

"I have to go out front and wait for the boss. Why don't the two of you have a friendly conversation, maybe chat about where you plan to go to dinner tonight?"

Giving us a friendly nod, Sol walked back the way we had come.

"Don't pay any attention to him," Mike said. "He doesn't understand what's going on. I'd try to explain it to him, but it's so complicated he wouldn't believe me anyway."

"Why don't you explain it to me?"

"I can do that in one word: starfish."

I leaned back against the post, stunned. "You're the person I was supposed to give the painting to if Mr. Peabody couldn't come back."

"That's right. I hired Peabody to buy that painting because I wanted to see who would try to buy it back from him. I figured maybe that way I could trace the whole art ring back to its source. Then maybe I would know who's been trying to kill me."

"Kill you?"

"I'm Dennis Rafferty. Pleased to meet you. I'd shake hands, but I'm tied up at the moment."

"You're Rafferty?"

"In the flesh. I disappeared to try to hunt down these people, but they got hold of a picture of me and grabbed me first. So much for doing a better job than the police."

"This isn't funny," I said. "These people have killed twice already."

"Twice?"

I told him about the death of Bernie Walker.

"Yeah, the boss was probably afraid that he'd talk in exchange for time off."

"Who is the boss?"

Rafferty shook his head. "That I don't know yet."

"How did you end up like this?"

"You mean tied up and helpless? Your friend, Sol, found me last night before I could change bed and breakfasts again. Bernie Walker's wife, Clarissa, was with him. She would happily have shot me with her little twenty-two if I didn't come along peaceably."

"She's here?" I said, feeling an emptiness grow in the pit of my stomach. "She probably thinks I killed her husband."

"Why would she think that?"

"It doesn't matter. So are you saying that everything you've told me so far has been a lie? You don't sell medical devices? You aren't being subpoenaed? You aren't worried about keeping your job?"

"My name is Dennis Rafferty and I'm a painter. The one true thing I told you is that I do live in Brooklyn."

"How did you know all that stuff about medical devices?"

"I have a friend in the field, and he likes to tell stories."

"What about being single? Was that a lie, too?"

"No, that was another true thing I told you."

"And why did you come in the gallery and ask me out?"

Rafferty stared across the room for a moment as if searching for something in the shadows.

"At first, I'll admit, it was because I wanted to keep track of what was happening with the painting. I thought maybe I could get some information from you about the two who tried to outbid Peabody. I figured if I could find out who they were, I might be able to trace them back to their boss. I never expected them to kill poor old Peabody. I thought the only person they wanted dead was me. But apparently getting that last painting was something of an obsession with their boss."

"So you went out with me as part of your detective scheme," I said.

"But I kept going out with you because I liked you. I wanted to break it off several times. I thought I should, because hanging around me can be dangerous. Look at how you almost got hit twice just because you were near me. But I wanted to keep on seeing you, even though you were more interested in that old boyfriend of yours."

"At least he didn't lie to me."

"Point taken."

"How did they get a picture of you?"

"Sol had one from a newspaper. It was taken several years ago. I've always been pretty careful to avoid publicity. I didn't even know that picture was out there."

"What's going to happen now?" I asked. I didn't really want to hear the answer because I thought I knew, and it wasn't going to be good.

"I assume the boss is going to arrive shortly to take possession of that painting. That will give him ownership of almost eighty percent of the paintings I've done. That's not as many as you might think because I'm not that prolific. I take a long time over each painting."

"Painting those up and down arrows takes time."

He laughed. "C'mon, you like the humor in my work, don't you?"

"I'm having a hard time finding anything at all humorous at the moment. So once the boss shows up, what happens next?"

"I think you know. He'll kill me, so that my work will appreciate in value. He'll probably try to do it in some way that makes it look like an accident or suicide. I'm afraid he will also kill you because you know too much. I wouldn't be half surprised if Sol doesn't go down as well, because he really isn't part of the gang."

We heard footsteps making their way over the creaky wooden floor. Sol appeared first. He had a sort of embarrassed smile on his face. Behind him was Clarissa. She held a gun pointed at the small of Sol's back.

Clarissa waved the gun toward the post where I was sitting.

"You sit behind her," she ordered.

Sol slowly got down on the floor. He put his hands behind the post, poking me in the small of the back, and Clarissa snapped on the handcuffs. Then Clarissa moved around the post and faced me.

"You killed my Bernie," she said.

I opened my mouth to say I hadn't, but she backhanded me across the face so hard, it brought tears to my eyes. Half in shock, I closed my mouth and didn't say anything.

"But you'll pay for that," she said.

Having made her promise, which left me almost hysterical, she marched across the room and disappeared into the darkness.

"I tried to tell you, Sol," Rafferty said.

"Yeah, I never was very good at listening."

"What can we do?" I asked, knowing I sounded desperate. But Clarissa's threat had about driven me over the edge.

"Let me try to slide around this post a little," Sol said. "If I can just get my hand in my back pocket, I might be able to help us."

I heard several grunts of effort behind me.

"Got it!" Sol said in triumph. "Now if you can just move a little closer to me, we might be cooking with gas."

I slid around until we were almost side by side. I felt a metal instrument slide inside the lock on my cuffs.

"Do you have a key?" I asked.

"Not exactly. But after fifteen years on the job as a cop, you'd expect me to have a way to open these things."

He twisted whatever it was around for several seconds, and suddenly I felt the left cuff spring free. I took my arms from around the post.

"Let me try to free the two of you."

"There's no time," Sol said, and Rafferty nodded his head in agreement. "Do you still have your cell phone?"

"Yes."

"Well, get out of here, and once you're safe, call the police," Sol said.

"Do it, Laura!" Rafferty said. "We still have time, but you have to get away."

I went back across the carriage house the way I had come in, on the alert for Clarissa, who I kept imagining in every dark corner lying in wait for me. When I got to the open barn door, I carefully peered outside. No signs of Clarissa or anyone else. I walked to my left, away from the old house, and hid behind a large bush. Slowly, going from bush to bush, I headed toward the street. I was about halfway there when I heard the crunch of feet making their way up the circular driveway. I peeked out through the leaves and saw Stephen, looking tired and out of breath, walking past me. I darted out from concealment and grabbed his arm, twisting him toward me.

"You've got to get out of here, Stephen. These people are killers."

He stared at me, annoyed and confused. I stared at him, frustrated by his incomprehension. He took a step back, twisting away from me, and by the time it clicked, his balled-up fist was already making contact with my face and everything went black.

CHAPTER 32

I was lying on my back, and a face loomed over mine. Slowly it came into focus, and I saw Sol staring down at me with concern. All I was aware of was pain. It extended from my head down the left side of my face.

"Can you open and close your mouth?" he asked.

That seemed like a foolish request, but I did it anyway.

"Good. Your jaw probably isn't broken. You might have a fractured cheekbone, and you're certainly going to have one hell of a bruise."

"Stephen is the boss," I mumbled.

"We know," Rafferty replied. "He carried you in and dumped you on the floor."

"That means that everything he told us—" I began.

"Was a lie," Mike said. "He was an even better liar than I am. He had my picture and knew who I was all along, and I thought he was just an overweight fifth-grade teacher."

"And he started going out with Angie just to stay close to me and the painting," I said.

"Never underestimate teachers," Sol said cryptically.

I realized that, while I was lying on the ground, my hands weren't cuffed.

"Why aren't my hands cuffed?"

"Because she's here," Sol said. I twisted around and saw Clarissa in front of us with a gun in her hand.

She smiled when she saw me look at her.

"You could have gotten away, but you're too stupid to live."

I shared her opinion of me. I should have figured out Stephen was involved rather than heedlessly running out to *save* him.

"Slide up against the post and put your back to mine," Sol said.

I felt something smooth and metallic slide into my hand. Clarissa had walked off to the side and was looking around, apparently not worried about us as long as she had her gun.

"Just keep poking around in the slot of my cuff. Eventually you'll trip the lock."

Looking straight ahead so Clarissa wouldn't suspect, I finally managed to get the tool in the key slot and did as Sol directed. Just as I was about to suggest that lock-picking took a special skill I lacked, there was a low snap and I felt his cuff spring free.

"Let me change positions with you, so she can't see my hands," Sol said. He shifted his butt along the floor as I slowly moved away from the post, continuing to block him from her view. Soon he was facing Clarissa.

"Can I go over and talk to Rafferty?" I asked.

Clarissa smiled. "Sure. But you'd better make it quick. Neither one of you has much time left."

I crawled across the floor and leaned my head against the post facing Clarissa. If she thought it odd that I wasn't facing Rafferty, she didn't say anything. Having the gun seemed to make her supremely self-confident. I started talking to Rafferty in low tones so she couldn't hear. I guess Clarissa thought we were exchanging terms of endearment because she made no attempt to stop us. Actually, I was directing Mike to put his hands where I could get at them. In a minute or two his cuffs were open as well.

"This is good," Rafferty whispered. "But it doesn't help us

much as long as she's got the gun. She's far enough away that if we rushed her, she'd have time to shoot at least two of us."

"But this may be the best chance we have before Stephen comes back," I said.

I looked over at Sol, who was watching me as if waiting for a signal to charge.

"I don't know why I have to be here. This has nothing to do with me," a querulous voice said behind me.

"If you want to reap the rewards, you have to be there for the dirty work," Stephen said.

I turned around and saw Stephen and Mr. Tompkins come into view.

"I never knew this was what you had in mind," Tompkins said, looking at the three of us. "This will be a massacre. We'll never get away with it."

Stephen smiled. "Don't worry. Sol and the girl's body will never be discovered. Rafferty's most certainly will be, but everyone will think he was the sad victim of a drug overdose, another artist who lost his grip on reality."

"Do we really have to kill them all?" Tompkins said, giving me an apologetic look.

"What difference does it make?" Stephen said. "Kill one or kill three, it's murder, and they can't execute you twice."

"You mean kill five, don't you?" I said.

"What's she talking about?" asked Tompkins.

"Well, there's the three of us, then Peabody and Bernie Walker."

"You killed Walker," said Stephen, sounding calm but getting slightly red in the face.

"Oh, sure. A big bad man like Walker let me waltz right up to him and hit him over the head."

I glanced at Clarissa. She was looking on with interest. I saw some movement deep in the shadows behind Stephen. I wondered if the FBI could have already followed me here. Clarissa didn't seem to have spotted it yet, so I had to keep her attention on Stephen.

"How did it happen, Stephen? Did Walker threaten to cooperate with the police? That's why you bailed him out, right? Maybe you told him you'd give him and Clarissa money so they could run away somewhere to avoid prosecution. Whatever you said, you gained his trust enough that he let you get close enough to hit him on the head."

"Stephen?" Clarissa asked. Her gun was now pointed in his direction.

"Don't believe—"

Brew charged out of the darkness with a length of wood in his hand and struck Stephen on the side of the head. At almost the same instant, Clarissa fired. Brew staggered for a moment, but got behind Tompkins. Clarissa's second shot hit the gallery owner, who dropped to the ground. By this time Sol, who was the closest to Clarissa, was charging forward. There was one more shot, but he kept going and managed to knock her off her feet. But then he lay on the ground. I was right behind him, and as Clarissa reached to pick up the gun that had fallen from her hand, I kicked it away.

In one fluid movement, she got to her feet, and the knife appeared. On the balls of her feet, she came toward me fast, the knife held out in front of her. I backed up until I slammed into a post. Clarissa smiled, and I saw her right arm go back as she made ready to lunge.

"Drop it!" Rafferty said, sticking the muzzle of her gun in her ear.

Clarissa reluctantly raised her hands, and the knife dropped to the floor.

I rushed across the room to Brew who was on one knee with blood running from his shoulder. He assured me he'd be fine.

"You didn't leave me," I said.

He gave a faint smile. "I never was good at knowing the right time to walk away."

Stephen was propped up on one arm, shaking his head as if trying to clear it. I walked up to him and, taking a giant step forward, kicked him in the groin, putting all my weight behind the kick. He screamed.

"That's for hitting me," I said.

I kicked him again, even harder. "That's for breaking Angie's heart."

CHAPTER 33

It was lucky that Clarissa preferred a small-caliber gun, because a lot of people got shot, but no one died. Brew had a shoulder wound that did no permanent damage.

Sol had been shot in the chest, but fortunately, no significant organs were hit. He was in a lot of pain from a couple of broken ribs, but otherwise he was okay. The worst case was Tompkins, who had an abdominal wound that required a long surgery and a slow and painful recovery, something we all felt he richly deserved. Stephen regained consciousness in the hospital, where he was diagnosed with a nasty concussion and a severely bruised groin.

After we called the police from the carriage house, we were inundated with law officers from both the local and the federal government. The FBI had been only a few blocks away, interviewing folks to see if anyone had spotted a white van. They would eventually have gotten to us, but whether they'd have been in time was hard to tell.

Over the next few days, I heard, mostly from Agent Ganz, who seemed to have taken a liking to me, that Stephen represented an eastern European crime family that had come up with the bright idea of buying up art and then killing the artist. If you ask me, there must be easier ways to make money illegally, although the Feds seemed pretty impressed. Stephen actually had taught fifth grade for a short time, an experience he described to authorities as the worst of his life.

Apparently Stephen had approached Tompkins because he needed a small but legitimate dealer to handle the Raffertys when they went on sale a few years after the artist's death. He'd found out that Tompkins needed cash, so Stephen offered to keep the gallery solvent in return for its future use. Tompkins has insisted he had no idea that there was any plan to kill Rafferty. Since it seems to be his word against Stephen's, he may get away with it, although he'll probably still do time for art theft.

Stephen wanted to buy one last Rafferty before killing the artist, so when one came on the market, he got Tompkins to buy it with the intention of selling it to his own people. That was where Rafferty and Mr. Peabody came along and fouled up their plans. Once Stephen recognized Rafferty, it was just a matter of time before Rafferty would die in some way that could be interpreted as accidental.

More important to me, personally, was the fact that the Tompkins Gallery immediately closed. Probably Tompkins figured he'd better start selling off inventory and the building as a way of raising money for his defense fund. That left me with bills to pay and no job.

Fortunately, I got a call that same day from Miranda, who told me that she and Harold had rented an empty store on the mall. They were going to open their own gallery, and she wanted me to work there. Two weeks later, when my face finally stopped looking like an out-take from *Night of the Living Dead,* I started working there.

So now I stand all day in a gallery with no actual art in it, since it is devoted solely to local artists doing nature painting. I will admit, however, that some of Harold's recent, non-bird works do have a certain appeal. Surprisingly, he does seem to have prospects as an artist. But whether the stuff I sell is art or not, it is a lot of fun working there, and it gives me an income for the rest of the summer.

What about after the summer? Well, that isn't exactly settled yet. When I found out that Mike, a.k.a. Dennis Rafferty, was an artist, I invoked my no-dating-artists rule. Rafferty tried to talk me out of it, saying he wasn't your typically childish, self-centered painter, and arguing that he was capable of having a mature relationship.

Maybe so, but it bothered me that he had lied to me so convincingly. In my experience, people always lie to you eventually about something, but most of the time they aren't very good at it and you can tell you're being lied to. But Rafferty was too good. I'd never be completely sure, when he told me something, whether it was the truth or not. That kind of distrust isn't a good foundation for any relationship.

So Angie and I are back where we started, two single girls with no dating prospects. It will take her a long time to get over Stephen, but I have seen her beginning to look with interest at the occasional handsome guy who passes our way. So I have hope for her in the not-too-distant future.

I said goodbye to Brew the other day. He came by my condo carrying his pack, much as he had arrived, except he was now on his meds. I wanted him to wait longer for his wound to heal, but he insisted he was ready to get back on the road.

"Well, it was sure great seeing you again," I said, knowing that sounded trite. "And thanks for saving my life, twice."

He grinned. "Who knew that selling art was such a dangerous occupation?"

"You see, you don't have to be in a war to get shot."

"Yeah, I seem to attract trouble."

We stood there for a long moment staring at each other, neither one of us knowing what we wanted to say or what we wanted to hear.

"I'd ask you to stay—"

He held up a hand, stopping me.

"I know that until I get the sound of distant guns out of my mind, I won't be of much use to anybody. I hope if I keep moving, one day I'll wake up and the sounds will be gone."

"I hope things work out that way."

He nodded. I reached over, hugged him and kissed him gently on the lips. Then I watched as he slung his pack on his shoulders and headed out the door. I watched him leave and kept watching until he was just a small dot against the background of the ocean.

ABOUT THE AUTHOR

Glen Ebisch has a doctorate in philosophy and has taught for over twenty years at a local university. He has been writing fiction for the same period of time, and has had more than fifteen novels published, most of them mysteries.

His interests include yoga, weight training, gardening, and reading. He and his wife live in western Massachusetts by the foothills of the Berkshires.